Deathly Alive

by

Lauren Bradley

DORRANCE PUBLISHING CO
EST. 1920
PITTSBURGH, PENNSYLVANIA 15238

Cover art by Brandon Stewart, titled "Wayward", created 2022, www.atramentstudios.com. Brandon is an exceptional artist, friend, and all-around excellent soul, and am forever grateful and honored to have his work grace our cover.

Dorrance Publishing Co
585 Alpha Drive
Pittsburgh, PA 15238
Visit our website at www.dorrancebookstore.com

ISBN: 979-8-88812-041-5
eISBN: 979-8-88812-541-0

Contents

Prologue - Risen

Madeliene awoke to the melodic sound of her neighborhood church choir. They were singing, "Ave Maria" which she had always loved, but for some reason today it sounded so incredibly sad and muffled. It was also strangely dark, and she could barely move because something soft, yet confining was holding her nearly immobile. Madeliene attempted to raise her hand to her face but could only feel silky soft material barely a few inches above her. As the song poured over her, people weeping could also be heard from somewhere nearby.

"Why did you leave me, Madeliene?" she heard her mother exclaim in the usual tone that always reflected anger more than affection.

Out of reflex, she replied, "I'm sorry, Mother!" but like in a dream, no one replied. Everything felt surreal, and for a moment she thought, *I must be dreaming...where you can hear someone, but no one can hear you.*

The choir abruptly stopped singing, and the music was replaced by the deep, rich voice of Reverend Josiah Rite. "We come here today on November second, in the year of our Lord, nineteen hundred and sixty-one, to support the family and friends of Madeliene Cross. A young lady, whom I had the pleasure of knowing as a good Christian girl but plagued by the darkness of the Devil."

The reverend's words shook Madeliene to the reality she was in a coffin...at her own funeral service! The shock sent her mind racing back to the last thing she remembered. A pain...a sharp pain in her chest, as her frail heart stopped, brought on after years of striving to be perfect, thin, and away from...something she could not remember.

At first, a combination of panic and confusion overwhelmed Madeliene. "After all," she muttered, "how can I possibly be dead and still hear everyone around me? Surely, someone at the hospital has made a horrible mistake!" She twisted back and forth frightfully and after a few tortuous seconds finally managed to pull her hands up to her chest. Motionless, she waited for what felt like an eternity, greeted by nothing but resolute silence from within; not a single heartbeat or breath!

Sliding her right hand farther up to her neck, Madeliene felt her favorite necklace and fingers fumbling past the fine, delicate silver chain. Her skin, however, was rigid and cold, which only added to her growing panic, but there was something else. Something had punctured her neck and created two small, but jagged, wounds.

It was at that instant, when within her a powerful force surged in an uncontrollable rage, causing Madeliene's senses to swell and then explode. "This cannot be real!" she exclaimed, pushing on the coffin's lid as it groaned loudly but held firm.

Reverend Rite stopped talking, and she heard several gasps from people outside of her tiny prison.

"They can hear me!" she rejoiced. Reaching down inside, Madeliene focused and pushed a second time, and the rigid oak lid groaned louder and buckled upward, still holding its seal.

Cries erupted from the mourners within the church when her third attempt broke the lid free of its seal and sent it crashing to the wooden floor, tossed aside like a child's broken doll. The ensuing panic sent everyone pouring out of the tiny neighborhood church with cries of "THE DEVIL WALKS AMONG US!" or "LORD HAVE MERCY!" as nearly fifty parishioners and well-wishers stampeded out the door.

Immediately rising to a seated position, Madeliene turned and glared, eyes burning with rage at the only persons remaining in the church: the stunned and wordless reverend and her controlling mother. She climbed lithely out of the casket remnants and approached her mother.

Reverend Rite reached instinctively for his Bible, but Madeliene felt his motions and her head snapped towards him, and commanded, "Don't even think about it, Reverend!" which stopped him motionless with fear. Turning back to her mother, staring in disbelief at Madeliene, she said, "I'm sorry to have left you, Mother," disdain filling her every word. "I know what a disappointment it must have been."

Her mother, still locked in shock, could only utter, "In God's name, I don't know what you are!"

Madeliene reached out instinctively and touched her mother's cheek. The older woman's gaze turned glassy at her daughter's cold and lifeless touch, as if in a trance. Madeliene said, "Think of me fondly, Mother; and I'm sorry I was never good enough to replace my father."

Madeliene then released her mother, glared one final time at the reverend before turning away and strolling quietly out of the church and into the crisp autumn evening.

Chapter 1 – Passing and New Moon

Everyone there on that fateful November night eventually moved on, either in life or death. Regardless of distance and time, none would ever manage to escape the mark it had left on their souls. Most folks moved far away within a year or two, but no one ever returned to that tiny church perched on a grassy Ozark mound by the river. Everyone there believed firmly that evil had touched their once blessed sanctuary and forever tainted the very grounds on which it rested. An evil so profane, some predicted it was certain to spread and eventually consume the entire community, if not forever abandoned.

With his flock disbanded to the winds, faith fatally crippled, and his beloved church facing eminent foreclosure, Reverend Rite committed an unforgivable sin. Two years to the night, he went to Jay's Hardware in town, purchased five gallons of kerosene, then rang the old church bells nine times before setting it ablaze. As the ensuing flames lit up the towering Cedar-shake steeple and leapt into the night sky, the former reverend, Josiah Rite, quietly slipped out of town, and was never seen again.

Decades passed in the tiny Ozark town of River Rock, but the events lived on, first as memories, then as folks moved away or passed on their story to the next generation; it grew into local folklore. Meanwhile, the small community of River Rock changed as people arrived from Kansas City and St. Louis to vacation and live in the fresh country air.

Delinda Cross, Madeliene's mother, never moved away from her modest home on Old Cedar Road. She also never really lived after that fateful day and would speak to no one of what had occurred in November 1961, no matter how hard some pressed her or gossiped. In her silence and building isolation, she eventually became known by many as "Crazy Cross," the woman driven insane by her rendezvous with the devil and hell spawn offspring.

At the age of ninety-five, her birthday, she too finally left town by passing away alone and quietly in her bed on Friday, April 1st, 2022. Delinda died a reclusive shell of a woman, surrounded only by her regrets and ever gnawing grief...or so it seemed.

Sitting on high forested ridge Old Cedar Road was the only county road that remained from the original town footprint, or Old Town as it was called in River Rock. Most of original town was built on low ground along the Osage River, which was bought out in the seventies and raised to make room for the new lake. When Old Town disappeared beneath the rising water, the new town of River Rock developed along the lakefront and built out eastward, leaving a fragment of Old Cedar Road and about two dozen homes isolated, the remainder reduced to an old overgrown trail that descended into the muddy lake waters. The once quiet, wooded, and picturesque country road, a main path of Old Town, deteriorated into a rundown remnant, impassible with dense overgrowth. Eventually, only four homes, scattered along that gravel road remained accessible and occupied year-round, the remainder became either seasonal lake homes or collapsed ruins, also reclaimed by cedars and thick overgrowth.

One of the occupied houses, only half a mile away from the Cross property at Nine South resided the Duncan family. On the opposite side of the road were the Baskins at Ten South. Both families moved in from elsewhere late 2013, a little over a decade ago, and had young sons who were the same age. The boys, Jimmy James "JJ" Duncan and Tommy Baskins, while complete opposites, became the best of friends and were now both eighteen and high school seniors. They also did the occasional favors for their neighbor Mrs. Cross, who lived at the end of Old Cedar Road. In her elder years, she had become frail, shut-in, and afraid to leave her home.

Saturday, April 2nd was a cool but mostly clear day. JJ woke to the all too familiar sound of his dad yelling into his attic bedroom.

"Get up, boy. It's almost ten, and you need to take Mrs. Cross her groceries we picked up last night."

JJ rubbed the sleep out of his eyes, glanced at his cellphone, and replied, "No problem, Dad. Mrs. Cross called me last night and said not to come by today. She's not feeling well." He rolled over to sleep a bit more, but his dad replied sternly:

"Jimmy James Duncan, get your rearend out of bed and take those groceries over to Mrs. Cross. I've got a delivery in St. Louis today, and your mom's busy with your sister in town. And check in with the Baskin boy—Tommy should have a load of cut wood for her."

JJ groaned out, "Okay, Dad, I'm up." Sitting on the edge of his bed, while rubbing the sleep from his eyes, he located his cellphone and immediately texted Tommy: *Hey I've got stuff for Mrs. C be by in ten K?*

Tommy replied in seconds: *Works for me, back the Camino up to the barn.*

JJ got dressed and put everything for Mrs. Cross in his dad's rusty old sixty-eight El Camino. Pulling into Tommy's driveway, he backed up to the barn in time to see his friend coming out with a load of split firewood in an overfilled wheelbarrow. He jumped out and gave his friend a high-five. "Big Tommy! Hear you got wood for Mrs. C."

Tommy, being a much larger and varsity offensive tackle, easily slapped JJ's hand away and replied, "That is so wrong!" while laughing with his friend.

The boys loaded the firewood and afterwards sat on the car's tailgate for few minutes.

JJ asked, "Any solid recruitments yet?"

Tommy replied, "A few. Coach and recruiter from MU came by the house last week. They offered me a full ride, so my parents are totally stoked."

"How about you?" JJ pressed.

"Oh, I don't care where I go. If I can play ball, I'm good. Besides, it keeps me closer to home in case my dad needs any help with the farm. I think Tracy is considering going there too, so we can both be Tigers." He cracked his neck and asked, "And what about you? Any letters come in the mail lately?"

JJ peered towards his place across the road and replied, "Letter arrived last week," he humbly responded. "Looks like I'm heading to Massachusetts in the fall."

Tommy grinned and gave his friend a celebratory high-five. "Nice going, JJ! Hey, buddy, be loud and proud. MIT was your goal, right?"

JJ nodded and said, "Totally. The moving away thing is unnerving for me, though."

"I get it. Honestly, the whole college thing weirds me out too. What about Ally? She made any decisions? I mean, you're not breaking up, are you?"

JJ replied, "Can't say at this point. I know she wants to get far away from her parents and has the grades to go pretty much anywhere. Journalism, maybe. Think she needs some more time to sort it out."

Tommy patted him on the back and said with a wide grin, "Well, at least by this time in the fall, no matter what, our parents won't be telling us what to do every day." He jumped down from the tailgate, stretched, and said, "Speaking of what to do, guess we better get over to Mrs. C's. As my dad would say, 'We're burning daylight.'"

JJ stood up, and replied, "You bet, Boomer," making them both laugh as they got into the car and sped off along Old Cedar Road.

Arriving at 29 South, they drove up the long gravel drive to Mrs. Cross house, exited their car, and walked up to front door. The old house had sure seen better days, and like the surrounding hollow had over years of neglect become so choaked with oaks, cedars, and honeysuckle it almost blocked out the morning sun.

JJ knocked on the front door and called out, "Mrs. Cross? It's Jimmy."

But there was no answer.

"Maybe she's still asleep?" Tommy shrugged.

"She keeps a spare key in the garden patio," JJ replied. "I'll get it and take the bags inside while you unload the wood. K?"

Tommy nodded. "Works for me." Then, in almost a whisper, "Honestly, her place creeps me out. I don't know why but I always feel like someone's watching me when I'm down here. Like now. Know what I mean?"

JJ surveyed the property and replied, "Her poor old place is like Mrs. C. Nice but beat up hard from time. I'll go get the spare key and let myself in. She's probably reading her Bible or something." JJ retrieved the key then glanced at his cell before opening the door. "Ugh, no service, as usual." Before going inside, he called out to his friend, "Hey, Tommy! Can you text Tracy and Ally? My phone's a brick today."

Tommy checked his, but it had the same problem, not even a bar of service. "No good, JJ. I'll finish unloading this and walk back out to the road. You can meet me out there after helping Mrs. C."

JJ nodded, turned the key, and opened her door. He knocked once more on the door frame and said loudly and upon entering, "It's Jimmy, Mrs. Cross! I'll put your groceries in the kitchen." After hearing no response, repeated, "Mrs. Cross?" and again nothing but the ticking of an old clock on the living room fireplace mantel. JJ shrugged and entered.

The house was nearly dark with only a few slender rays of daylight filtering between dusty, closed living room drapes and dirty windowpanes. Not unusual for Mrs. Cross, who wasn't exactly the best housekeeper, but today it oddly smelled damp and felt cold. He reflexively flicked the light switch, but power seemed to be out. So, he placed her groceries on the kitchen table and checked her landline; it too was dead. "Figures," JJ muttered to himself. He called out once again for Mrs. Cross but, as before, she did not respond.

Working his way cautiously down the small hallway to the back room, he noticed the bedroom door on the left was ajar and peered inside. "Mrs. Cross... Oh no!"

Mrs. Cross's lifeless body lay in bed, her head slumped forward. JJ quickly glanced around the room, then carefully felt the woman's extended, frail, and cold pale wrist for a pulse. Nothing. He was about to go back outside when he noticed something unusual. It was a tiny, grainy, black and white photograph of a young Mrs. Cross holding a baby; stained and curled with age, resting on the floor having slipped from her fingers now dangling from the edge of her bed, no doubt after her passing. Kneeling briefly to pick up the photo, JJ said a silent prayer for Mrs. Cross but as his gaze rose, he met the old woman's lifeless eyes.

Now, JJ had seen both of his grandparents die at the hospital, so while tragic, an elder's death was nothing new. The sight and smell were sadly all too familiar to the young man. But this was something different. Mrs. Cross's lifeless face was etched in absolute horror, cloudy eyes wide, and rimmed with blood.

It startled him back to his feet, where he ran out of the house, jumped into his car, and sped out, throwing gravel everywhere and nearly spinning out into the nearby pond before regaining control and returning to where Tommy was standing and texting on his cellphone at the end of the driveway.

"SHE'S DEAD, TOMMY! OH MY GOD, SHE'S DEAD! CALL 911!"

Thirty minutes later, Deputy Benjamin Talon from the Benton County Sheriff's Office arrived. The deputy wrote down JJ's initial statement, checked the home, and a few minutes later returned and called it in. "Dispatch, Deputy Talon...10-54 confirmed at 29 South, Old Cedar Road. Need to contact the sheriff and county coroner and send them out here ASAP. I'll secure the property until they arrive." He turned back to the teens and said, "Best go home, boys. Nothing more you can do here. I've got your statements; if we need anything else, we'll call you."

As they left, Tommy drove the car instead because JJ was too upset. To break the uncomfortable silence, Tommy said, "It's almost noon. I told the girls we'd meet up in town at Picky's and get some pizza."

JJ only nodded in silence. As they were driving away, he felt something odd in his pocket and pulled out the old photo of Mrs. Cross and the baby. "That's weird," he muttered to himself out loud.

"What is?" replied Tommy.

"I found this old photo by Mrs. C but didn't remember putting it in my pocket...guess I was pretty freaked out. I mean, how else did it get there?" He turned it over and on the back was written: *Madeliene, October 28, 1945*. He read the name and date to Tommy but mispronounce the name "Made-linee?"

Moments later, his cellphone pinged in a voicemail. JJ instinctively checked the message and dropped his phone to the car floorboard, which made Tommy jerk the steering wheel.

"JJ, what's up with you, man?"

To which JJ replied, "Tommy, pull over!" while retrieving his cellphone.

Tommy stopped the car while JJ played his voicemail on speaker. A distant, young feminine voice said only one thing in almost a whisper: "Madeliene."

Chapter 2 – Dream Walking

As close as JJ and Tommy were, Tracy Hillman and Ally Denton were even closer. They were next-door neighbors in town and had been best friends as far back as anyone could remember, having both been born in River Rock. Tracy was the county sheriff's daughter, and Ally's dad was pastor at the First Baptist Church of River Rock. All four teens had become inseparable in high school and perfectly made an odd pairing. Tommy and Tracy were classic ballers and fit each other like a pair of gloves, whereas JJ was a quiet kid who could speak code even in the most seasoned geek-speak forum. A natural tech wiz and hardcore gamer to the core. Ally was the dreamer of their pack, who played the "good-girl" image for her parents and their church group, but kept a journal and dreamed of becoming a writer far away from her smalltown roots.

When the guys finally showed up at Picky's, the pizza had already gotten cold. While initially annoyed at their boyfriends' usual tardiness, the serious expressions on their faces made them forgive and turned to concern.

"So, your text said Crazy Cross was dead, but you actually found her?" asked Ally.

To which JJ replied, "Totally, dead...and don't be mean, Ally. She was only lonely or something. Mrs. C was always nice to me and Tommy."

Tommy added, "Yeah, now show them the photo and play the voicemail."

JJ did, and the girls both shuddered in disbelief.

"Okay, that's freaky. I've even got goosebumps. Wait a minute. Are you guys messing with us?" Tracy asked, skeptically eyeing the guys.

"I wish," JJ replied.

"So now what?" asked Ally. "I mean, seems like you found that picture for a reason, right?"

JJ shrugged, while Tommy rolled his eyes, sighed, and replied, "Oh, not the legend, again…"

Ally retorted, "It's not like I believe it, of course, but you must admit today was weird. At least a six on the Weirdlandia Scale," she blurted, and added, "Maybe there's something more to find out?"

Tracy said, "Hey, I know. My dad's probably there now. I can ask him later about it."

Ally added, "And I can check around at church tonight too. It's Saturday and the church elders will all be there; a couple were as old as Crazy—ah, I mean, Mrs. Cross."

"Hey, all we need now is a groovy van, a big dog, and we could be like that old cartoon my dad watches," Tommy said, snickering. Bad joke, but it broke the somber mood. "Well, I need to get back home. Got Saturday chores to finish or dad will 'nail my hide to the wall,'" he added, making quotation marks and smiling.

As they all got up to leave, JJ said, "I'll poke around online. Maybe I can find out something about the old photo and Mrs. Cross's family. My dad has an account with one of those *Ancestor* deals. Must at least be a birth certificate or something out there. I'll DM everyone later if I find anything useful."

They all nodded in agreement.

As they were leaving, Tommy asked, "Tell me, you guys aren't going to leave all the pizza?"

Ally replied, "Yes, it's cold and gross."

Tommy replied with a wink, "Nah, it's pizza. Good for at least a few days, I figure," and, smiling, went to get a box for the leftovers.

Tracy rolled her eyes and said to Ally and JJ sarcastically, "Great, it seems my boyfriend is Shaggy," which made them all laugh.

Later that evening, JJ was successful online at finding Mrs. Gundelinda Cross's birth certificate: born in Stokkvagen, Norway April 1st, 1927. The website also located her first US census in 1940 at age thirteen, maiden name Flett, and her marriage license to a Thomas Cross, dated April 26, 1944. JJ also located Mr. Cross's veteran service record and their daughter's birth certificate, DOB October 28, 1945.

Madeliene was her name. He thought the photo must have been taken on the day she was born. But then he located her father's death certificate: "DOD, March 3rd, 1945, killed in action in Stuttgart, Germany."

JJ paused and said to himself, "Man, her husband was killed six months before their daughter was even born. No wonder she was so sad. Then to tragically lose your daughter too."

JJ continued searching the website for records from the Old Town and local paper articles but couldn't locate any photos of Mrs. Cross, her husband, or their daughter beyond the one discovered at her home. He texted the others and waited.

Tommy responded first, but didn't know anything new, only saying: *Chores, dude...nothing new here.*

Tracy responded: *OMG so sad...still waiting on dad to get home let you know tomorrow, fingers crossed emoji.*

Ally texted last: *More news from Weirdlandia here, let's meet up tomorrow afternoon after church.*

JJ turned off his laptop and told his parents and little sister, Lena, goodnight. Once he was back in his room upstairs, he was closing the window blinds but stopped. For an instant, he thought he saw someone, maybe a darkhaired girl in old-fashioned white dress, standing by his car in the moonlight. He blinked but she was gone.

Racing downstairs and outside, he tripped his parent's motion lights which lit up the driveway. But found no one. He shrugged, muttering himself, "Not like some girl is going to be hanging out, watching for me anyway."

A few seconds later, his dad came out of the house armed with his shotgun. "Boy, what's going on?"

JJ replied, "Sorry, Dad, thought I saw something moving by the car from upstairs."

His dad searched all around and said, "Well, couldn't have been anything too big, didn't trip the lights. Probably a coon."

JJ replied, "Must be. Sorry, Dad."

Then a light breeze shifted from the west and an odor of reeking decay made them both back away towards the house, coughing.

"Holy crap on a cracker!" his dad exclaimed, pulling his T-shirt up over his nose and mouth and pointing towards the house. "Let's get inside! Smells like rabid skunk, and we darn sure don't want to find it in the dark!"

Back inside and upstairs, JJ glanced at his cellphone one last time for the day. It was now almost midnight, and exhausted from the day's events, he eventually drifted off to sleep.

At least until his cellphone texts started chiming in after three a.m. from his friends. Each saying in all caps:

WE NEED TO TALK!

Finally free of family and her Sunday obligations, and thanks to Ally feigning illness to miss her dad's usually longwinded sermon, the teens met up at the place where no one in town visited on Sunday mornings. The town's old library.

Mrs. Griffin excitedly greeted them with a smile. "You kids showing such strong scholastic interest has truly made my day a blessing. Besides the professor over there from Washington University working on some research project, you will probably have the place to yourselves all day." She pointed towards a neatly dressed elderly man oblivious to their presence and pouring over stacks of books, maps, and notes on a nearby table.

After Ms. Griffin was out of hearing range, JJ started first, telling them everything he had found online and what had occurred in his driveway the previous night.

Ally was next. She had asked a couple church elders about Mrs. Cross, always leading for sympathy at her recent passing. Most, unfortunately, wouldn't even discuss it or didn't know anything specific other than the usual gossip. However, she learned one of the elders, and oldest at ninety-eight, Mr. Jay Turner, knew Mr. Cross.

"I like Mr. Jay," Tommy interrupted. "My dad said he used to run the old hardware store before the lake was built, then a big box bought him out later. He's a good guy and always sponsors our sports clubs."

Ally nodded in acknowledgement. "Mr. Jay is nice and was the only elder who would say anything to me at all. He said Mr. Cross was from a local family and had met Mrs. Cross a few years after the war broke out. She was a young immigrant from Norway, and they met at a soldier's dance back east and fell deeply in love. After they married, she was soon pregnant and moved back here, since he was shipping out to Europe, but took his death hard and never remarried.

"He also said she was too tough on their daughter, whom he remembered as a quiet but polite girl. She was homeschooled, though, so other than at church or occasionally at the grocery store, no one in town ever really saw either of them. When I asked about her daughter's death, he completely shut down and said it was best to let some things stay in the past."

She subsequently pulled out her journal and opened it to a drawing, a small stack of rocks overgrown with honeysuckle. "I had been journaling last night, like I do most nights. But when I woke this morning, my journal was open and this drawing was in it," she said nervously. "I can't draw like this. Not this good."

Tracy was next. "I spoke with my dad. He didn't get home until after nine o'clock last night. I could tell by the exhaustion etched on his face it had been a grueling day. When I asked him about Mrs. Cross, he got quiet and said it was still an active crime scene under investigation. When I pressed him, he said the county coroner will tell us more later, but for now it was being listed as suspicious because it didn't appear natural."

JJ injected, "The sheriff doesn't think Tommy or I had anything to do with it, does he?"

"No...at least, I don't think so. Dad said she died early, likely hours, before you boys showed up. Don't worry, the county coroner is my favorite uncle. I'm sure I can get him to tell me more later, but that's not the weirdest part." Tracy pulled a small sandwich bag with a bunch of long black hair out of her purse. "My mom makes me brush my hair every night, one-hundred strokes before bed, so it's always on my nightstand. I'm obviously blond, and no one in my family has long dark hair. Something woke me up around three a.m., like someone whispering in the bathroom. I walked in there, found my brush sitting on the sink full of this, and when I glanced up at the mirror, I swear a teenage girl was staring back at me with dark hair and pale skin. Startled, I jerked away, but in a blink, she was gone."

Last, they all turned to Tommy who had been listening quietly. "I went home, did my usual chores, ate all the leftover pizza—man, that was so good—then slept like a baby," to which the others groaned in aggravation. But he added, "At least until around three a.m. when I woke to sound of...well, I don't know what. I thought it was a cat outside. But it didn't sound right, like it was sick or hurt. Figured it was another feral cat that probably got hit by a car. Anyway, I never saw it, but when I opened my window, man, the stench about knocked me over. So, like JJ and his dad, I closed the window and waited until this morning to see what it was. No cat, no more smell, but it left little pawprints all around my house in the dirt."

Ally said, "So, a smelly, feral cat was around your house last night and that's weird how?"

Tommy replied, "The ground was dry this morning, Ally. It hasn't rained in days. Heck, I weigh almost two hundred and eighty pounds and was barely making a dent in the dirt. How can a cat leave pawprints everywhere I can't? Makes no sense. And the smell—I've never smelled anything that bad. I mean, once I even left my gym bag in the truck over a hot weekend after the game with Ozark, and even it didn't smell that bad. It was plain unnatural."

Ally said, "Then what's going on? I'm drawing in my sleep, something I've never seen before; Tracy has a ghost or something using her hairbrush that maybe visited JJ, with a smelly animal that travelled over to Tommy's place too. Or am I the only one who's officially freaking out here?"

Their brief silence was interrupted by the elderly man nearby. "Have any of you ever heard of 'dream walking'?"

The teens scrutinized the stranger but said nothing as he approached their table.

"I'm sorry to interrupt your discourse, but it seemed, well, interestingly familiar to dream walking."

JJ asked, "Sir, what is dream walking? And aren't you a college professor?"

"Again, my humble apologies for interrupting, and a tad bit of eavesdropping, but yes, I'm a retired archeologist and anthropologist. My name is Dr. Daniel Tombs, professor emeritus, you know, and my field of study is early Native American cultures, especially here in the Middle Americas. These cultures are full of stories regarding dream walking, which are spirits that can cross over from spirit world into ours, usually during our dreams. Good news is, they're typically harbingers of goodwill or simply trying to be helpful by leaving bits and pieces of information through dreams, spirit drawing, and spirit animals but sometimes they also manifest strong physical emanations, odors, and occasionally leaving behind physical impressions. At least that's what the stories say."

"Why do you think this might be something Native American?" asked JJ.

The professor replied, "Sounds strikingly similar, that's all. And this area has deep roots dating back over thousands of years to ancient native cultures. That's why I've been visiting all the town libraries throughout the state pouring over old maps for anything that could have previously been native structures. For instance, the Cahokia mound builders were well-established east of this area over a thousand years ago. I've always suspected their influence stretched farther west of the Mississippi but, unfortunately, most of the ancient structures were either buried by time or simply pilfered and destroyed by Europeans later."

Tommy started to uncontrollably chuckle, and the others stared at him strangely. "Come on. Am I the only one who gets this? His name is like Tombs, and he studies old dead people."

Tracy glared at him, eyes rolling, while JJ and Ally groaned in dismay at their immature, and rude, friend.

"The big guy is right; my name has been a good joke for many a student over the years, and I certainly don't take it personal," he added with a wink to Tommy. "Tell you what," he said, reaching into his tweed coat pocket, "here is my card and number. I'll go back through some of my past research to see if anything specific comes mind; meanwhile, if you do find anything significant that could be Native

American in origin, please call me." The professor returned to his table and continued with his studies.

JJ then said quietly to the group, "I know what to do next. Ally's drawing resembles a place in the back of Mrs. Cross's garden."

Chapter 3 – Dark Omens

The teens dropped off JJ's car at his house and piled into Tracy's black SUV her dad let her use since he always drove his sheriff's truck instead. By the time they arrived at the Cross home, it was almost four p.m. The warm morning sun had since disappeared behind a blanket of thickening grey clouds, making the cool April day feel dreary and heavy. Tracy parked the car at the end of the drive beneath a walnut tree, they slipped under the police tape and walked along the thinning gravel drive to the house.

JJ asked Ally, "Don't you need to get home before your dad and mom find out you're not really sick?"

Ally replied, "My parents are always at church on Sunday until well past six." She smiled and pointed her index finger to her cheek. "Besides, if they do catch me, I'll say I was feeling better, but you were so upset and really needed a friend today. Daddy always buys it 'cause I'm his good girl, you know," she added with a sly smile and giggle, while intentionally foundling a little golden crucifix on a light chain around her neck.

At the house, JJ pointed out a slender cobblestone path that wound around the side. The overgrowth of honeysuckle vines made the path narrower than it should have been and required them to walk single file with JJ leading the way.

Tracy asked, with a tone of concern, "Why aren't the vines blooming? I mean, they're almost everywhere else in town by now. Weird, right?"

Tommy answered, "Probably too thick back in this hollow to get enough sunlight. Nothing weird here to see Tracy, only plants."

Tracy stood briefly still, shuttered, and asked the group quietly, "Does anyone else feel like we're being watched?"

Tommy responded, "For sure. I get that feeling every time I come here too."

Exactly as JJ had told them earlier, the path opened behind the house into a small garden. It was built into the natural limestone terraces, but also matched the rest of the Cross property, overgrown with vines and covered in deep piles of dead oak leaves and cedar needles from the surrounding woods, which emitted a damp and musky smell. The hand-laid stonework and dead vines were also sporadically covered in a fuzzy, blueish-grey moss.

"Man, I bet the rats like it back here," Tommy said reflexively, to which Tracy responded by punching him in the shoulder, exclaiming:

"EW! You know I hate those things!"

Ally's gaze scanned the area. "I think this was once a fairy garden. See; there's a little gnome statue here poking out of the leaves, and one over there too, and an old water well." She brushed away the rotted forest debris to reveal a small pitted, concrete gnome holding a water pail and small garden shovel; paint dulled and peeling away from its tiny face and body. "It was probably cute back here once."

Tracy said, "GROSS! Don't pick that up, Ally. Who knows what's been crawling around it."

Ally giggled at her friend's visceral reaction. "It's a cute little garden gnome. Little beat up, sure, but I think they're supposed to be protective or something."

Tommy joked while swinging his arm in a shoveling motion. "Yep, they whistle while we work."

JJ, meanwhile, had been brushing away thick piles of old leaves and needles in one of the stone terraces when his boot hit something hard. He pushed another pile of debris away revealing three larger stones stacked neatly together but intertwined by several dead vines and more blueish moss, exactly like Ally's drawing. "Found it, Ally!" he exclaimed, carefully reaching through the vines until his hand felt something soft like leather. "Tommy, get over here and lift the rock on top."

Tommy jumped up on the terrace next to JJ. "On it," and grabbed the large cap stone. He lifted it effortlessly, which allowed JJ to retrieve a small, weather-beaten notebook inscribed with the initials "M.C." He brushed away the stray pine needles and debris before handing it to Ally. Once more, JJ reached back inside the hidden space, recovering three old flint arrowheads and what resembled a small, polished river stone marked with a strange inscription: "ᚱᛗᛈᛗᛟᛗ."

Tommy set the large capstone back down once JJ was clear. He peered over his friend's shoulder at the artifacts in his hand, and said, "Arrowheads. Nice score, JJ! Bet that professor would pay a few bucks to get these." He patted him on the back. "Maybe you can get the Camino painted now—I'm thinking candy-apple red."

JJ replied, "Maybe, but this other stone is bizarre. I mean, see how the arrowheads are cool to the touch, flint probably, but this stone is warm. And these things belong to Mrs. C... I mean, *belonged* to her. We can't steal them."

Tommy said with a shrug, "I don't think she cares anymore, JJ, and I figure finders keepers. But if it makes you feel better, take a couple pics and put them back. I'll slip the rock back in place and push a few leaves over it. Seems safe enough for now."

Ally was busy flipping through the book and exclaimed, "Tracy and I need to borrow the book! I think it's a journal. We can read through it tonight while you guys call that professor and send him the pics."

Tracy sighed loudly. "Ugg! Can't tonight, Ally. School night, and you know my mom won't let me miss pool time in the morning before classes."

"It's okay," she replied. "I'll read through it tonight and catch up to you at lunch or homeroom tomorrow if I discover anything interesting."

Even though it was well before sunset, the sky had become darker than usual. Stray clouds that preceded their trespass had become threatening and warned of an impending spring storm. Feeling the winds shifting and beginning to strengthen, the teens decided it was time to leave while the sudden absence of sunlight made the vine-choaked path almost as dark as night.

They were leaving the garden when out of nowhere a roar of thunder clapped directly above them, issuing a bolt of lightning that struck the very terrace they had been standing on seconds before. The hidden place flashed with a bright violet light and explosion, causing them all to scream and instinctively turn away. Seconds later, they glanced back finding the little stone structure had been charred, but the moss on the dead vines now glowed with an eerie, ember-like intensity.

JJ, ever fast with his cellphone camera, was able to briefly capture the image before the spectacle faded away. They subsequently ran back to Tracy's car and sped away.

Tracy stopped in the roadway between JJ's and Tommy's homes to let them out. The storm was getting stronger, so the boys quickly waved them on.

When the girls drove off, JJ said to Tommy, "I think I'm officially with Ally in being freaked out now. Let's go to my house and see if the professor can tell us anything."

But the bigger teen said, "You go ahead and I'll catch up a in few. Need to go home first and check in with my parents and probably change a few things." He smiled. "Never been that close to lightning before in all my life and, man, I'm pretty sure it didn't rain in my shorts back there!"

JJ smiled and, feeling better, replied honestly, "Didn't want to say it in front of the girls, but I really could use a shower too."

Tommy later returned to JJ's house, conveniently in time for dinner, as the rain had started to fall heavily from the pitch-black sky. After supper, the teens dashed up to JJ's attic bedroom to "work on a school project" for few hours, carefully using the exact story Tommy had told his parents.

JJ said, "Sorry about my kid sister creeping on you throughout dinner."

Tommy laughed. "No big thing. I mean, Lena's like ten, right? Probably the football thing, 'cause chicks dig ballers."

JJ replied, "No, probably the muscle thing, 'cause she has a brother who virtually has none."

Tommy instinctively stretched, flexed his large biceps, and said, "Maybe, but my muscles are big on the outside, and the ones inside that head of yours are like massive, my friend."

That made JJ smile. "Yeah, massive, for sure. Now let's ring up that professor." JJ pulled the contact card out of his wallet, set his cellphone to speaker, and called.

"Hello?" a familiar voice answered.

"Professor, this is Jimmy Duncan and Tommy Baskins calling. We met at the library today."

"Ah yes, Mr. Duncan and Mr. Baskins, what can I do for you gentlemen on a rainy Sunday evening?"

Tommy replied, "Well, sir, you said if we found anything unusual to call you back. Well, I think we did."

JJ added, "Sir, we found some artifacts not far from our homes. I'm sending you the pics as we speak."

The professor responded, "Alright, the images are here; let's see what we have." After a brief pause, "Oh my goodness. These arrowheads are most definitely Cahokian influenced. Do you have them, by any chance?"

JJ winced. "Well, kind of."

Tommy then asked, "Hey, professor, what about the stone? It's Caho, Cahok, ah, Native American?"

Dr. Tombs replied, "Definitely not Cahokian, but the image is too blurry for any detailed analysis. It almost resembles a Nordic runestone of some kind. But I'm not at all certain, nor am I an expert on that topic. If you wish, I can forward it to a colleague of mine back at Wash U."

JJ said, "That would be great, professor."

Dr. Tombs added, "I've been examining a few of the old town's maps before the lake was built, and may have stumbled onto something interesting. If you have time later this week, please stop by the library where we can chat and compare research. And if you have those artifacts, I'm certainly available to evaluate them further."

JJ replied, "Sounds good, professor. I'll check in with the girls and see you later this week. Thanks again, and goodnight."

Tommy asked, "JJ, why didn't you show him the light show?"

JJ was staring down at his phone and then held the pic up for Tommy. "It's that weird stone. The pic is blurry, and I know it was perfectly clear when I snapped it."

Tommy shrugged. "Maybe the lightning zapped it or something?"

JJ flicked through his pics quickly. "But it's the only pic that got fuzzy… I mean, check this out." He played the video of the glowing moss; it was only a few seconds in duration.

Afterwards, Tommy said, "So? I was there too."

JJ backed up the video with his fingers, slowed the image, and then paused it. For a millisecond and between flickers of moss light, a hazy image of young girl with a flowing white dress and dark hair was staring at them in the garden.

Tommy's phone inconveniently buzzed and quacked with his duck text tone, making them both jump. He glanced at the message. "Texts are from Dad. Rain's getting heavier, so I need to get home. See you tomorrow, JJ."

He nodded as Tommy started to leave. "Hope Ally will have more tomorrow at school." While listening to the rain, he added, "Don't melt, Tommy."

Tommy added with a chuckle as he was leaving, "Heck, I don't melt, 'cause poo dissolves."

Tommy was always a natural athlete and, despite the driving rainfall, easily cleared JJ's place in a few seconds. He let out a youthful roar, having a bit of fun, when he stopped roughly five-hundred feet from his house. The rain whipped around his stocky, muscular frame as he stared out into the darkness, but there was something moving slowly nearby and pacing him. He wiped away the rain from his brow, squinted, and yelled, "WHO'S THERE?"

In response, something in the darkness bellowed a deep-throated snort, like a bull. The noise was followed by a familiar stench that washed over him, exactly like last night. His nostrils immediately burned and eyes watered, Tommy nervously considered whether to run to his house or the barn. The barn was closer. A breath later, the sky issued a thunderous crack and flash of lightning which lit up the pitch-black night—and he saw it.

"CRAP!" Tommy exclaimed in terror, turning and running to the barn as fast as he could. Heart pounding, he could hear the beast behind him, larger than a pickup and baring down; massive hooves clapping in the rain and mud, with a thunderous snort that once again breathed the familiar vile smell. He narrowly made the doorway, pivoted, and abruptly slammed the heavy oak door shut, dropping the thick security bar in place.

A split-second later, the beast collided with the barn. The impact was so intense it knocked Tommy backwards on the ground as the barn's heavy wooden barricade held but buckled inward. Meanwhile, his family's horses whinnied and the pigs in their pen squealed nearby in terror, kicking and biting feverously at their stalls to escape.

Between claps of thunder, the beast snorted loudly once more as it struck the barn a second time. The second collision rattled every timber in the structure, but miraculously held together while Tommy crouched in fear at the building's center.

He could hear it once again snorting and ferociously pounding the ground in rage, and then it struck a third time. The impact lifted the entire barn off its foundation, walls buckled in, and the loft collapsed inside, sending heavy searing timbers flying and raining downward within the failing structure.

Suddenly, a clap of thunder rang out, followed by a blinding, violet display of lightning striking the ground, outside of the barn door where it leapt and ripped through the roofline, making the beast wail in anger and retreating off into the darkness.

All the animals were silent. As quickly as the maelstrom started, it ended. In its wake, leaving only the soft, pitter-patter of a light spring shower, and Tommy curled up on the ground, battered, bleeding, and in a shock-driven frenzy surrounded by nothing but piles of burned and twisted timbers where his parents eventually found him.

Chapter 4 – From the Ashes

JJ's mom gently woke him while sitting on the side of his bed. "Honey, wake up."

He stared up at his mom lovingly, then with concern after seeing her expression. "Mom, what's wrong?"

"It's Tommy, honey." Jerking himself upright, his mom held her hand to his chest. "Sandy called me from the hospital. He got hurt last night going home in the storm and is in surgery now. Ray asked your dad to go over to see if any of his animals survived. Said it was a microburst that hit the barn on his way home. Thank God Tommy was able to take shelter."

JJ jumped up and quickly dressed, before racing outside and over to the Baskin's place. Running up the long gravel driveway, he spotted his dad with Sheriff Hillman walking around the shattered remnants of the barn. There were only a few fragments of the original building that remained standing. Everything else was either leveled or in twisted heaps.

"Dad!" he yelled, running up before his dad's thick arm stopped him.

"Whoa, boy! It isn't safe to go in there. The barn's broke all to hell, at least what's left of it."

JJ stared at the destruction in disbelief. It appeared as if something had hit it so hard it lifted it completely off the ground, leaving all four walls shattered inward. There were also six great gaping holes on the front and a massive, jagged burn mark on the ground out front that etched up and over the roofline, cutting it completely in half.

"What about animals?" asked JJ.

Sheriff said, "Both horses died in their stalls, likely electrocuted from the lightning strike. Pigs got crushed under the loft when it caved in too. Best we can tell, Tommy was standing in the center of the barn when it got hit. Probably the only thing that saved him. Must have been an angel watching over him last night, for sure, because if he had been standing anywhere else, Baskins would be planning a funeral today." The sheriff patted JJ on the shoulder, and said to JJ's dad, "I'll stop by the hospital, check in on him, and give a copy of my report to his parents for their insurance." He shook his head. "Darn shame; it was a nice barn, but thank God the house didn't get hit too."

The sheriff slipped into his patrol car. As he was pulling away, he stopped briefly and added, "JJ, Tracy doesn't know yet. So, do me a favor and don't text her. At least until her mom can pick her up from swim practice in about thirty minutes. Okay?"

JJ was still staring in disbelief at the barn, nodded, and replied obediently, "Yes, sir."

***

Later at school, JJ found Ally before first hour and could tell she'd been crying. Naturally, Tracy never made it to school but texted Ally she was at the hospital in Clinton with Tommy.

JJ hugged her and said, "He's going to be alright; I know it."

Ally shook her head and said, "I stayed up almost all night reading... It's her journal; Madeliene's. Let's meet up at lunch and talk." She anxiously inhaled a deep breath. "I'm really scared, JJ. I think we've stumbled onto something dark...maybe even evil."

Time seemed to almost stand still while JJ nervously fidgeted at his desk throughout his morning classes.

When the third hour class bell rang the end-hour chime, JJ bolted out of class, through the usual maze of students, and down the hall into the cafeteria. Ally was already there, her class being closer, but to his amazement, so was Tracy, her eyes also red and watery. JJ gave her a hug and said, "Shouldn't you be at the hospital or home?"

She defiantly shook her head and said, "They don't know if Tommy will ever walk again because a couple timbers struck him on the back."

JJ squeezed her hand supportively. "But your dad said he'd be alright," he told her, grasping for some hopeful news.

"Doctor said his spinal cord was severely bruised and, truth is, they don't know for sure. The neurosurgeon said it could take weeks or even months because the spine is slow to heal."

Ally interjected to help change the subject, "Tracy, tell him what Tommy told you."

She nodded, pushed back her tears, and said, "Tommy was heavily sedated and in recovery when I got there. After a few minutes, he briefly came to while I was the only one in his room, and started to shake all over. I tried to comfort him, but Tommy suddenly grabbed my wrists, eyes wide with fear, and said, 'Tell JJ the smell was a beast—huge, skinless, and black as night.' It had come for him, exactly like in Daniel 7.7, but at the last minute, she somehow saved him."

JJ asked, "She? Who saved him?"

Tracy leaned in closer to her friends and whispered, "Madeliene. Tommy told me she appeared directly above him, right as the barn was collapsing. She somehow shielded him from most of the building. Her cold hand briefly touched him tenderly on his left cheek and whispered into his ear, before disappearing into the storm and leading the beast away. He then slipped back into unconsciousness. When his mom returned, I had to get here...to warn you both."

"Warn us of what?" asked JJ.

Tracy shook her head and replied, "I don't know! Everything is crazy! Madeliene said, 'Beware the Split Moon,' and the skin on Tommy's left cheek is blueish-black and raw. Doctors couldn't explain it but said it's frostbit where the tissue instantly died. It may need to be removed later today to avoid an infection." She glanced nervously back to Ally. "Read it to him."

In response, Ally produced a small Bible from her backpack which she always carried, and read: "'After this, as I watched in my vision in the night, suddenly a fourth beast appeared, and it was terrifying—dreadful and extremely strong—with large iron teeth. It devoured and crushed; then it trampled underfoot whatever was left. It was different from all the beasts before it, and it had ten horns.' Daniel 7.7."

JJ sat back and tried to let everything sink in. After a few seconds, he turned back to Ally. "Dare I ask what the journal said?"

"She wrote it in her last year. Her life must have been a living hell, and her mom was completely mental. She pushed her daughter to be the perfect Christian, the perfect girl, free of sin. Continually berated her for having 'Old Blood' and being susceptible to the 'Deathly Alive'."

JJ asked, "What does all that mean?"

Ally replied, "I don't know, and Madeliene didn't say in her journal. She also wrote how badly she wanted to be like the other kids in town, able to go anywhere and be with friends. But her mom would never allow it. Her life was church and home. She couldn't take it anymore and slowly starved herself to death, hoping to make it all stop. Her second-to-last entry was made the day before she died."

Ally read them the passage:

"'He watches me constantly. Every time we go to church, I can feel his gaze upon me, more and more. When I was little, the Reverend Rite was always there, ever watching, but like a father I so missed having in my life. He used to make me feel safe and I thought he was nice. But now he unsettles me to my soul. The way he looks at me has changed since last year, especially when he thinks I'm not watching. He and Mother talk often but always far enough away that I cannot hear them. I feel lost and so alone. I begged Mother at summer's end to help me, but she only rejected me further with scornful displeasure at my *lustful and wicked thoughts*. How can wanting friends make me lustful and wicked? I feel colder every day and can't seem to wear enough clothes to stay warm. My hair has become painfully brittle, and it stings to run my brush through it. My heart sometimes beats so fast my chest hurts and makes me dizzy.

"'I tried one last time and prayed Sunday, after church, on my knees in the garden until they bled, but God remains silent and, like Mother, indifferent to my suffering. For what reason, I do not know. I long for a friend, for love, for dreams without the darkness that cloud my soul. To be honest, I'm jealous at times of the other kids in town. Maybe that is why God is silent and now my sin to bear. How wonderful it must be to have parents that love them. I no longer believe Mother knows how, and even blames me for Father's death.

"'I also fear her condemnation of me regarding the Old Blood is coming true. I heard it first in my dreams in early April. By mid-summer, I sensed something wicked began following me everywhere. Always lurking out of sight but leaving me feeling, at times, cold and nervous, and always watching. It started around the church grounds but more often occurs at night and seems to get nearer to the house, invisibly stalking me with a foul odor of death that burns my eyes.

"'A month ago, I finally caught a glimpse of it, from my bedroom window. It resembled a cat, so dark it was nearly blue, strolling calmly in our driveway under the pale moonlight. But suddenly, it froze, turned almost instinctually and stared directly at me, eyes void with light. In a blink, it shifted like a shadow from my sight and bolted away into the forest, sounding like a huge, beastly bull that snorted with a violent roar, leaving behind a trail of shredded brush, snapped saplings, and even uprooting a few mature cedar trees. How could a small cat do something like that?

"'Terrified, Mother visited town the next day, bought more garden gnomes, and placed them all around the house. Oh, how I've always hated those things since I was little. She said God would protect us, like in the old country, and keep the Deathly Alive away, but still, they unnerve me. But it's closer now. So close at times Mother and I dare not venture even into the garden anymore. I guess Mother's gnomes are silent too because she is also frightened. I stay locked in my room at night with the window drapes closed, while Mother paces around the house and prays nonstop. Something unnatural is coming for me, and I fear even death will not let me escape it.'"

Ally stopped reading and added, "Her last entry on the following page is from the day she died. It only said she planned to hide her journal out of fear her mother would burn it, along with 'her secret treasures' she found under the church's crawl space last spring. Her last sentence said, 'I fear the Deathly Alive and the Rev.'"

JJ asked, "Reverend Rite?"

Ally replied, "I don't know. Her sentence abruptly ended. Maybe her mother interrupted, or she knew she was dying and had to stash the journal."

JJ said, "Wow, her mother really had control. Too bad she didn't leave instead of starving herself to death."

"You have no idea what caused her to do that!" Tracy blurted, startling JJ and Ally. "You're lucky and have no idea what it's like having a mother who controls everything you do or eat. Tells you to be perfect or that you're not cutting it, no matter how hard you try." She gazed towards the cafeteria window. "Sometimes starving yourself..." she paused to roll up her left volleyball jersey sleeve she always wore, revealing dozens of thin scars from multiple razor cuts; some old and pale but a few more recent, "...or worse. It's the only thing you can control."

Ally hugged her friend tightly. "I didn't know. I'm so sorry for whining all the time about my dad being controlling. Does Tommy know?"

Tracy nodded. "He's always there for me with his stupid jokes but never judging, and I love him dearly. To think something hurt him intentionally, and Madeliene too, makes me—"

JJ interrupted, grasping her left wrist in support, "Want to kick its evil butt," which made Tracy smile through the tears.

"Yes! But where do we even start?" she sighed. "No one is ever going to believe us. Not even my dad would believe us. I mean, I wouldn't have believed us last week."

Ally said, "Maybe your uncle can tell you more about Mrs. Cross and why her death is listed as suspicious. I have youth group after school, but the church elders are meeting again too. Thought I'd try one more time with Mr. Jay, and ask him about

Reverend Rite. JJ can also call the professor again, and maybe we can meet up with him tomorrow at the library after school?"

Ally and JJ nodded in agreement, right as the class bell rang for fourth hour to start.

***

After school, Tracy was back in the pool. As much as she hated gymnastics, soccer, basketball, and track, swimming was her escape. In the water she could get lost in her thoughts, and best of all, not have to hear her mom because she never stayed for swim practice.

The other five girls on the team had been exposed to Covid last week and were quarantined at home, leaving the pool all to Tracy; the boys didn't get it until four-thirty. Nothing but the cool water all around her and the lovely rhythmic release. Water was always her true friend. On her final lap, as aways, she pushed hard and, once finished, pulled herself up, out of the pool and lay down on her back to catch her breath. The cool, moist concrete felt reassuring as she closed her eyes to relax for a few minutes. Morning had been so early and maybe she could squeeze in a quick nap, she thought before drifting off.

While she slumbered, the pool lights flickered three times before shutting off. In the dark, a fine mist rose off the water, eventually filling the room with a moist, cool fog.

Tracy unconsciously shivered and began to wake when something extremely heavy violently landed hard on her chest. The pain snapped her awake, but her arms and legs oddly could not respond; her body rigid and locked motionless in place. It required everything she could muster to even open her eyes and tip her chin forward. Her efforts, however, were greeted by a horrific odor and blackish-blue, shadowy thing sitting on her chest. She tried to scream, but the pressure baring down on her breastbone barely allowed her to utter even a whisper of, "No…"

The thing seemed to turn around, almost cat-like at times, revealing two black eyes void of life and burning with rage. As she gasped for air, it felt as if her chest was collapsing from the sheer weight of the creature. Tracy was nearly unconscious when something extraordinarily cold grabbed her arm and, with tremendous force, pulled her into the water, causing the beast to bound away and wail in a sickly, cat-like growl.

When she broke the water's surface, the lights had come back on, the mist was nearly gone, and so was the beast. Tracy held tight to the pool's edge, coughing and slowly regaining her breath.

Finally able to get out of the pool, she ran into the locker room to quickly gathered her things. Slipping on her shoes and grabbing her backpack while still wrapped in a towel, she began to leave, shaking in fear from the assault. As she reached for the handle, Tracy turned twice, feeling like something was there, watching, outside of her vision. When she turned back a third time, she froze; there was now the image of a young girl with black hair in an old-fashioned, faded white dress staring back at her from within the nearest mirror, shadowy eyes laced with sadness.

Tracy stiffened and asked hesitantly, "You're Madeliene, aren't you?"

To which the girl only nodded wordlessly. The spirit then stared at Tracy's left arm, at her scars, and Madeliene smiled with an expression of complete empathy.

Tracy tried to approach the mirror, but Madeliene timidly backed away at her sudden advance, to which she pleaded, "Wait... Please," and Madeliene moved back, closer, revealing to Tracy a dark set of gaping punctures in her pale neck.

"I'm so sorry, and thank you for saving me and my Tommy."

Madeliene smiled again, then stared off beyond Tracy as if she sensed something in the distance before grimacing in an expressive mix of fear and anger.

Tracy said firmly, "We are your friends and will help you!"

Madeliene stared once again at Tracy as tears rolled down her face, a smile returning, and said sadly, "He will never let me go." In a blink, she was gone.

Tracy regained her thoughts, ran out to her car, and immediately texted Ally, who did not respond. "Oh, she's at the church by now," she said to herself in frustration and drove straight home.

***

Ally, meanwhile, was able to slip away from the youth group at church and into the rectory hoping to find Mr. Turner. Luckily, she found him outside the kitchen getting a cup of coffee, and smiled.

"Evening, Mr. Jay."

The elderly man smiled kindly and replied, "Evening to you, Miss Denton. I heard about the Baskin's boy. So awful. I pray to God he'll make a full recovery."

Turning on her best preacher's daughter charm, she replied, "Thank you, sir. Tommy's a good friend and he's hurt pretty bad." Sensing the elder's concern, Ally pivoted and asked, "Sir, I hope I'm not talking out of place, but ever since Mrs. Cross passed away, some of the kids at school have been saying strange things, that, well, are scary." She carefully pulled her Bible in close, as if she were clinging to it for support, while drawing on the elder's sympathy.

"Oh, don't believe those old wives' tales; they're a lot of superstitious hogwash," he said, making a motion with his hands to let it go.

Ally, sensing an opening, pressed further. "I heard Mrs. Cross lost her husband in the war and her daughter had some troubles," to which Mr. Turner only nodded in agreement. "It really made me sad; although, some kids at school said the former reverend may have been inappropriate and that's probably why he burned the church down and left town suddenly."

The elder bowed his head and shook it from side to side, and retorted firmly, "No, Miss Denton! Whoever said that is simply wrong. I wasn't a member of his church in those days, but I knew Reverend Rite to be a good man. Not perfect, but decent. I don't know exactly what happened that night in 1961. Wasn't there. But something made everyone..." briefly going silent in thought, he sighed deeply, "...made Josiah go insane. I met Josiah Rite as a young theology student in Springfield, but I dropped out and moved back here to help my ailing father with the hardware store. It was a better fit for me anyway. Josiah was a good friend of mine throughout. After graduation, and at my suggestion, he moved here because River Rock was a small town without a church." He smiled at Ally. "If you can imagine that. Well, even as a Methodist minister, he fit right in and was the sort of man who made himself available anytime needed. Kind of like your father, which is why I was drawn to his church and evangelical preaching in these difficult times."

"Do you know what happened to him?"

Mr. Jay fidgeted uncomfortably, then replied, "He bought the kerosene from my store, but I had no idea what he was going to do with it. I knew he wasn't the same man—broken in sprit and faith by God knows what. After he left town, I'd hear from him from time to time; a call occasionally or he'd send me a postcard, usually during the holidays. Nothing specific, but it seemed as if he was searching for something and racked with guilt but would never tell me what it was."

"I'm very sorry. If I'm not being too forward, is he still alive?" asked Ally.

"Yes, he's still alive. Well, at least in body. His mind is pretty much gone; Alzheimer's took care of that, I'm afraid. I've always respected his privacy over the years, so I see no need to violate it today. I know he is being well cared for in St. Jam—" Then, cutting himself abruptly off, "Hopefully, what I've told you will calm your friends' gossip for good."

He glanced at his wristwatch seeming irritated at himself, and set down his now lukewarm cup of coffee. He said politely, but firmly, "I think it's time for this old man to go home. Goodnight, Miss Denton. Please give the pastor and your mom my best."

***

Mr. Jay walked back to his modest home, less than a block away from the church. His house was dark, which was odd since his lights were on a timer and the rest of the homes on the street were well lit. Fumbling for his keys, he found the front door locked, turned it, and strolled inside. Mr. Jay lived alone, because his wife had passed away a few years ago and his daughter lived in Kansas City with her family. His only companions at home were his birds—pigeons he loved and raced with other birders across the state. Trying to focus his eyes in the dark, he cooed, but the birds were silent. Mr. Jay tried the light switch, but the room remained dark.

"Don't worry, my little friends, must have popped the main," he said to his pets to calm them. Reaching into entryway vanity drawer, he found his flashlight and walked into the adjacent kitchen and opened the service panel. He reset the main breaker, but the lights did not come back on. "Guess I'm calling Pete out tomorrow to check our wiring, but until then, don't worry, I'll get the candles to keep you warm tonight."

Mr. Jay opened the kitchen silverware drawer and pulled out a small lighter and pack of votives, and walked back into the sunroom to his birds. He cooed again. "Sorry about the lights, my friends, but it's candles and blankets for us all tonight." As he set the candles and lighter down, he shined his light on the pigeon coop. Instead of resting in the dark in their roost bedding, all six of his prized racing birds were huddled together in back corner of their coop.

"Oh, my Lord, what's got into you tonight?" he exclaimed, shining his flashlight around, expecting to find a furry intruder.

Seconds later, the birds suddenly squawked fearfully, feathers flying about as they pushed away from him, even tearing at each other, desperately trying to stay in the back of the coop.

"What on earth has you so flustered? Stop! Calm down or you'll hurt each other!"

His last words were greeted from behind by an overwhelming stench of decay that burned his eyes, causing him to drop his flashlight while something powerful and vile moved towards him the dark.

***

By the time Ally got home, it was well past nine p.m. She dashed straight up to her bedroom and closed the door, uttering to herself, "Finally." She checked her cellphone and seeing Tracy's text: *IT CAME AFTER ME!!!* immediately called her.

"Tracy! My God, are you alright?" she asked, worried. "I'm coming right over!"

Tracy's voice was oddly reassuring. "Ally, I'm alright. Bruised, sore, and super-pissed but alright. Don't come over. My mom suspects something's up but, fortunately, Dad got a disturbance call in town and had to leave. She thinks I've gone to sleep, so let's tag JJ in and figure out what's next."

Ally reluctantly agreed. While they texted, she opened her journal and captured the day's events before the details could slip her mind.

Chapter 5 – The Lost Prophet

JJ, Ally, and Tracy texted well into the night. JJ had earlier contacted Professor Tombs, who said he could meet them at the library after school. After exchanging events that occurred to Tracy, and what Ally had learned from Mr. Jay, they agreed to ditch school by calling each other in sick. They also planned to meet up at the Foodmart over in Warsaw, where JJ could leave his car without someone from town seeing it. The plan was to first drive over to St. James, as Mr. Jay had let slip while talking to Ally, and hopefully find the former reverend, then drive back through Benton County and stop by the county coroner's office where Tracy's uncle was the local medical examiner. Lastly, they would stop by the town library in the afternoon and meet up with the professor.

It was another grey morning with the occasional mist, the kind enough to make the windshield messy with streaks. They loaded into Tracy's SUV, left Foodmart's parking lot, and drove to St. James.

Tracy asked, "So how do we find him? And, if we do, how can we get in to see him?"

JJ replied, "Well, according to Ally, Mr. Jay said the former reverend has Alzheimer's. So, while I was waiting on you this morning, I searched online for the nursing homes in St. James. There were only three and called asking for a Mr. Josiah Rite."

Ally said, "Nice going, JJ. Any luck?"

He smiled and said, "First two were a bust, but the last one said they had a Joe Rite in their memory care unit."

"As for getting in, I have an idea," Ally added, producing her Bible and two others. "Follow my lead when we get there."

Two hours later, they arrived at the Gleaming Oaks Retirement Community in St. James. Passing out the extra Bibles to her friends, they walked inside and approached the front desk, with Ally taking lead.

The staff member on duty stared at them, a stocky, gruff man with bad teeth, who asked dryly, "Visiting family?"

Ally replied with a sugary sweetness that made JJ suppress a laugh. "Why, yes, sir. We're here to see my cousin, Mr. Joe Rite."

The man scrutinized his computer screen and replied bluntly, "Nobody is listed on his guest or family list."

Ally responded, "He's my daddy's cousin, Pastor Denton over in River Rock. As kids, we always knew him as 'Poppa Joe,' but he's been sick for some time, and Daddy asked me if I'd bring a few friends from our youth group over to pray with him for healing."

The man smiled, his gruff demeanor softening. "Well, isn't that nice. Alright, I'll need to see your driver's licenses to put a copy in our guest roster."

Ally smiled and said, while pulling out hers, "Of course and thank you, sir."

Once they were in the system, the attendant said, "Mr. Rite is in the memory care wing, through the doors and down the left hall in room number nine."

"Thank you again, sir, and God bless you."

He nodded and pressed the buzzer allowing them inside past the locked security door.

They located his room, number nine, and slipped quietly inside. Mr. Rite was lying in a hospital bed, secured with restraints, and bordered with bed rails to prevent him from falling. The elderly man was awake but staring out the room's lone window into the distance, oblivious to their presence.

JJ asked, "Mr. Rite?"

The old man scratched his nose in response, seemingly lost within his own existence. Only the sound of a local news program on the television filled the room. He shook his head and said, "The lights are on, ladies, but I don't think anyone is home."

Ally moved beside the bedridden shell of a man and said, "Reverend Josiah Rite, we need to ask you about Madeliene Cross, please."

The effect her words had on him was immediate. His vision cleared and he turned his head towards Ally as if reciting a sermon. "I moved to River Rock in 1950 and began preaching the Gospel for anyone who wanted to listen. The town was small but had potential with so many hardworking good Christian folks. Thanks to my friend and local businessman, Jay Turner, I was able to secure a bank loan to buy a twenty-acre parcel, along the river and began gradually building our church and a foothold for our Lord. We dug the foundation over a small hill, on higher ground, since the river channel was but a few hundred feet away. After a few months, my church congregation grew to a dozen families and, within two years, the church was finished with over twenty families. Delinda Cross and her young daughter were part of my flock, my responsibility, you know...but God knows I failed them both."

"Can you tell us about it, please?" Ally asked. However, he became silent and only turned away. "Sir, something evil is still there. We think it killed Mrs. Cross this week, almost killed one of my friends, and now is after us. Reverend, it smells like death."

He faced Ally once again and said, with pain etched across his face, "As prosperous as the early fifties were, the latter half of that decade was difficult. Rains came and the church flooded several times and badly damaged the foundation. It cost so much to repair, and we were close to defaulting on the banknote. In spring of 1960, after the third washout and repair, I spotted Madeliene slipping out from under the crawl space. When I asked her what she had been doing, she mentioned hearing a cat, thought it was hurt, and crawled under there to investigate but didn't find one. She was dirty and obviously hiding something in her pockets, but I didn't push and figured she'd eventually tell me if it was important.

"That night, however, I was praying for God to help me find a way to save the church, when I smelled it and felt the cold, forbidding presence, for the first time. It spoke to me from the shadows, like in a vision; it showed me a cave in the mound, the walls lined with arrowheads and ancient pagan stones, with the symbol of grand knot, laced in twine reeds above the door. The presence told me to sever the knot and swore our church would be saved from the evil it had been built upon.

"Desperate, I brought a flashlight and crawled under the church. In the very back, I discovered a narrow rupture in the rock that must have been uncovered after the last flooding. It had sunk into the hillside. I had to squeeze myself to get through, but once inside, I saw exactly what the vision had shown me earlier. When I found and cut the knot above the old stone doorway, it slid opened and a dark presence stood before me, emitting that godawful smell.

I thought it was the angel of death itself and fell to my knees, praying for salvation. But instead of taking my life, it reached out a decayed, armored hand and dropped several silver ingots before me, and said, 'You have served me well. In repayment, your church will never succumb to the elements, so long as I am free. I only have one more request.'"

Again, he stopped speaking, as if searching for the words, prompting Ally to push, "What did it want?"

He shut his eyes in regret and said, "The thief stole something that was mine. She bears Old Blood, and therefore, is mine alone to judge or claim. I condemn her to the Deathly Alive. Forever tied to my spirit and this place for eternity."

Tracy's demeanor and rigid posture reflected how upset she was with the old man's confession. "You knew it was coming for her! She was terrified and begged for help and all along you had sold her out for silver."

"Matthew 26:15…" he said in bitter response, "I was her Judas, yes. The day Madeliene died, I wept, thinking perhaps she would be at peace, but then…three days later, it violated her corpse and two nights later, she rose. I tried to find her again but couldn't, and the entity beneath my church never permitted me access to its lair, even after I tried." He showed the teens his left arm which was horribly disfigured and scarred, as if something had nearly peeled the flesh away. "So, at last, I cast it into the everlasting fire and buried the cave under the church ruins. Twenty years later, the lake was built, and God cleansed away the evil I had released upon this world for good."

"Except he didn't," Tracy said with a glare. "My boyfriend almost died two nights ago, and may never walk again, and yesterday it came after me. It's after all of us. But you can still help Madeliene before it's too late."

He starred at her in disbelief. "You've seen Madeliene?"

Ally grasped the man's hand. "We all have had some encounter with her."

"Then I can only serve to warn you. Delinda, her mother, was always concerned for her daughter's safety. She was old world, superstitious and kept things around from her home country for protection."

"Like garden gnomes?" asked JJ.

To which the reverend nodded in agreement. "Yes, exactly. She believed to some degree in pagan spirits, something she also called the 'Old Blood' and felt the gnomes were their protectors, along with her strong Christian faith, of course." He focused on Tracy and said, "Judge me however you wish, for I surely deserve worse, but please do not judge Delinda too harshly. She wasn't much older than any of you when she got married and gave birth to Madeliene. When she moved to River Rock, the Cross family wasn't very welcoming either; her being an immigrant who spoke little English at first. A few years after her husband was killed in the war, they basically cut her off socially and, sadly, she couldn't afford to move back home. For all her faults and burdens, I know she loved her daughter, through private admissions."

"We still need to help her!" demanded Tracy.

He shook his head emphatically no. "Whatever has presented itself to you and your friends over the past few days, and what I saw in all those years ago, was not Madeliene Cross. She is no longer of the living and hasn't been for over sixty years. Worse, she is probably bound to whatever was beneath my old church in that dark place underground. Nothing good can come from an evil so profound. Surely, I am testament to that very truth.

"Even before her death, there was something else... Madeliene was not always as innocent as she appeared." After a brief pause, he fumbled with an object inside his gown and produced a small, delicate key from a chain around his neck, offering it to Ally. "Things are getting confusing again, so please take this before I forget. Delinda left it with me for safekeeping the night I burnt the church down. Maybe it can help you see things more clearly...Ave Maria...her dresser..." His gaze shifted back to the lone window as he slipped away in thought and lost forever beyond their words.

Ally asked, "Reverend? Reverend? What does it go to?"

But he no longer responded to them.

She snatched the small key before an attendant entered seconds later.

"Morning, Mr. Rite, how are we today?" Noticing the teens, said, "Jerry at the front desk said you were here to pray with Mr. Rite. Good thing family came by. Sorry he's not very communicative these days."

JJ said, "He was talking with us for a while but stopped a few moments ago."

She responded, "Really? Mr. Rite hasn't spoken to anyone on our staff for several months now." She checked his vitals. covered up his chest with the blanket for warmth. and added, "But that's how these things are sometimes. Nice he was able to break out and chat with you today, though. Your prayers must have helped." The staffer turned off his television and pulled the window drapes partly closed, darkening the room, turned on a small radio for music on the Reverend's side table, and said before leaving, "Best say your goodbyes for today, kids. Mr. Rite always likes to nap in the afternoon and doesn't seem to be up for much more activity today."

The teens followed the staffer out of Mr. Rite's room, closing the door behind them, all unaware of Madeliene's reflection had appeared on the television's screen, glaring intently at the former reverend, while the music from the radio turned to static.

Tracy, JJ, and Ally stopped in Warsaw, grabbed a sandwich and some coffees at a small diner before driving over to the town square and the Benton County Coroner's office.

Tracy walked inside to see her uncle, while JJ and Ally finished their coffees in the car. The grey, misty April morning sky had once again darkened, bringing more rainfall that nearly drenched Tracy while she ran into old red brick building.

Less than twenty minutes later, she reemerged, dashing back and jumping quickly in driver's seat. Her long blond hair dripping water down her sweatshirt, which she pulled back out of her face, and breathed deeply in thought while wiping the moisture from her face.

Ally, growing impatient, and fumbling with the mysterious key the reverend had given her, asked, "Well? Did your uncle tell you anything?"

"At first, nothing, but after a few minutes he admitted Mrs. Cross's death has been ruled a homicide; she was suffocated. Something heavy had been placed on her chest, breaking several ribs and left a large, circular frostbite burn. Sounds familiar," she added while instinctively rubbing her chest.

"So, we were right," Ally said. Then, sensing her best friend was holding something back, asked, "What else did your uncle say?"

Tracy started her car, turned on the windshield wipers, and turned up the defroster to clear off the steam building up on the back window. "Uncle Mike was called back to River Rock this morning." She turned towards Ally in the passenger seat. "It was Mr. Jay," which made Ally flinch, knocking her purse onto the floorboard and spilling its contents as she held her hands up to her mouth in shock.

Tracy added, "Uncle Mike said, in almost thirty years as coroner, he'd never seen anything so gruesome, like straight out of a horror movie. He wouldn't tell me anything specific, except to go home because his day was going to be a long one."

Ally bent over to recover her belongings, and said fearfully, "It's getting worse, isn't it?"

JJ interjected to change the conversation, "It's almost two o'clock. I think we need to get back and have a long conversation with Professor Tombs, but let's first make one quick stop."

Ally stared at her boyfriend in disbelief. "Surely, JJ, you aren't thinking what I think you're thinking."

JJ nodded. "We need to return to the Cross home. I think we've missed something important and maybe we can figure out what that key means or opens." He checked the time on his cellphone. "School will be out by the time we get back to town. Let's get my car and see if we can find some answers."

***

Less than an hour later, they were back at Mrs. Cross's place. JJ retrieved the hidden key and let them in, but they had to use their cellphones as flashlights since the power had been shut off.

As their eyes adjusted, he motioned in the direction of the hallway. "Bedrooms are at the end of the hall. Mrs. Cross's room is on the left."

Ally asked, "Then Madeliene's must be on the right?"

JJ shrugged. "I guess. Mrs. Cross never let me in that part of the house. Well, at least until I found her Saturday."

Tracy gazed around the room and into the kitchen, making a disturbed face. "This place resembles those gross, old black and white shows my dad watches on cable."

JJ nodded. "Yep. I never saw Mrs. Cross throw away anything. Even her old oven and fridge, or 'old goldies' my dad called them. I think he fixed them for her at least three or four times."

Ally pointed out multiple crucifixes and several Bibles, all tabbed with ribbons and dogeared from years of use, scattered around house. "No knickknacks or family photos?"

Tracy added, "More creepy gnomes, though. See, exactly like in the garden. Right by both front and back doors. Tommy always said this place gave him the jitters, now I know why."

JJ led them down the hall. He first tried the doorknob on the bedroom to the right, which was locked, and then to Mrs. Cross's bedroom, where the door was open. Things had obviously been moved around, likely from the police investigation and having to remove the body. Seeing the dresser, JJ walked over and slowly began opening the drawers filled with old clothes and other personal things he really wished he hadn't seen, when he uncovered a heavy wooden music box. The lid was hand-carved cherry ornate with the image of two songbirds in a nest, and at the base, a tiny keyhole. He carefully removed the music box and sat it on the dresser.

Ally was already beside him with the key. She inserted it into the keyhole, a perfect fit, and turned it. A small *click* of hidden latch was heard, and the front of the music box opened, revealing smaller hidden compartment filled with six letters, envelopes browned with age, and a separate envelope full of old, grainy black and white photos. The letters were postmarked between late January and most of February 1945.

Ally reminded them, "He said we should read these. And here, see," she added, lifting the lid on the music box, which began playing "Ave Maria" and made JJ instinctively shiver.

Tracy, however, had backed away from them, and replied matter-of-factly, "I don't trust anything he said. None of us should. I mean, for God sakes, look around this place!" She pointed. "No photos of her daughter anywhere. But hey, she's got more gnomes by the door and window to keep her safe... That worked out well." She snorted in sarcasm. "Ally, remember Madeliene's last entry in her journal?"

Ally replied, "'I fear the Deathly Alive and the Rev...'"

Tracy nodded. "Exactly! 'The Rev,' as in Reverend Rite. That low-life creeper sold her out and did nothing while her twisted mother made her days a living hell. You read them if you want, but I'll have nothing to do with those letters." She glanced at the time on her fitness bracelet and said resolutely, "I think we've been here long enough."

Ally patted her friend on the arm and replied, "It's okay, Tracy. JJ and I can get the things from out back while you wait in the car. It will only be a minute...or two." She paused, staring past her girlfriend into the hallway. "Wasn't that door closed?"

JJ spun around and said cautiously, "And locked."

The door to the opposite bedroom was ajar and the room beyond forbiddingly cloaked in darkness. JJ grabbed the envelopes before joining the others as they slipped hesitantly into the hallway, illuminated only by their cellphones, and pushed the door open to allow their meager lights to shine inside.

The room was starkly simple and painfully disturbing. Meager furnishings composed of an old twin bed covered with a musty and stained quilt, a small child's vanity, reading lamp, and closet still adorned with a few conservatively plain dresses worn and riddled by age and moths. The dust was so thick, it was apparent the room had never been entered for decades; wallpaper stained with age, peeling, and curling off in places.

Ally walked up to the bed and knelt to touch two worn impressions beside it. "This is where she prayed. See the marks and the dark brown stains." She shook her head aghast. "Oh my God...this is worse than I could have imagined."

"Told you guys," Tracy bragged, feeling vindicated.

Ally got up and walked over to the little dresser. "This is something you would buy for a child today, not a teenager. I'll never complain about anything ever again." She rubbed the decades of dust off the attached mirror before abruptly freezing, eyes wide in fear.

Tracy and JJ could see her too. It was Madeliene's image in the mirror and staring back curiously at Ally.

Ally started to speak, but the spirit interrupted, putting her finger to her lips and expressed quietly, as if in a library, "Shoosh." Madeliene whispered, "He's coming. Don't let him get my treasures. Quickly now," she added, staring up at JJ.

It was getting windy again outside, which made him jump. "I'll grab them and meet you at the cars!" he exclaimed while dashing down the hall and out the backdoor into the garden.

Tracy knelt beside Ally and pleaded with Madeliene, "Is there anything we can do to help?"

Madeliene smiled and replied, "The split moon is almost here. If he isn't gone by then, he will be freed on the nine, unstoppable and immortal." She stopped and glanced back over her shoulder, as the reflection of her room was fading from view and turning dark. "I'll tell you everything, tonight, where he cannot find me, but I can find you."

Ally asked, "What do you mean? Where?"

However, the darkness in the mirror behind Madeliene began to boil. In the distance, a vile, commanding voice uttered obscurely, "Gamall Blar, Gamall Blar, you will be mine... All will be mine!"

Tracy shouted in warning, "MADELIENE!"

Madeliene's eyes darkened, irises rippling with violence. She smiled at the teens and said, "Remember, his weakness is water!" The spirit spun away from the girls and screamed in anger, causing a violent bolt of lightning to erupt from her in all directions back towards the darkness as she commanded, "NOT MY FRIENDS!"

The mirror flashed in violent reflection as Tracy intuitively grabbed Ally and pulled her to the floor as it exploded, showering the room with tiny glass shards.

Unhurt and helping each other to stand, fine dust from the room and glass setting everywhere, they ran out of the house where the winds had also slowed down and found JJ frantically waving them into his car.

***

An hour later and back at the River Rock Library, the teens found the professor at what had become his usual table, still covered and overflowing in a pile of old maps and books. He was accompanied this time by another man in his late thirties with sandy, curly hair and a pleasant smile, casually dressed in a plaid shirt, jeans, and jean jacket.

After exchanging greetings, Professor Tombs introduced the other man as Dr. Walter McAdams, an associate professor of international studies, whose specialty was in modern and ancient Scandinavian culture, and something called geomorphology.

He smiled at the teens politely, and added, "Call me, Augie."

JJ started off their conversation by asking, "Professor Tombs, you mentioned stumbling across something important?"

The older man nodded and unfurled an old land survey map from 1892 which showed the original outline and land plats at the town's origin. Pointing to a hilltop symbol along the former Osage River basin, he said, "This symbol is nothing more than a mound, but what is interesting is the surveyor's note penciled in beneath."

It read: "Indian Mound."

"It was so small I had missed it before. Mesoamerican culture in this area, especially Cahokia mound builders, commonly built structures along waterways since rivers were common points for transporting goods in their day. And those arrowheads you found are strong evidence to support Cahokian influence. When you sent me those photos, I checked these old maps a second time and there it was."

"Coincidently," JJ said, reaching into his backpack and producing an old cloth he laid on the table and unrolled, revealing the three arrowheads and small symbol stone, charred from the prior lightning strike but unbroken.

The professors stared in disbelief at the teens and then excitedly picked up the artifacts.

Professor Tombs said, almost giddy with excitement, "These are absolutely Cahokian or, more precisely, Algonquin affiliated, flint works...appear to be around late 900 or maybe 1000 CE."

Ally asked, "Is that like AD?"

Professor Tombs lightly smiled. "Exactly, Ms. Denton, but with a secular twist."

Meanwhile, Professor McAdams had picked up the small stone and, turning it over in his hands, evaluated it using a small hand lens he had produced from his pocket. "Daniel, do you know what this is?" he said with elation. "This is an old Germanic runestone! And the inscription 'ᚱᛗᚹᛗᛟᛗ' is a series of binding words...collectively means 'vengeance.' It is absolutely from the same timeframe as the arrowheads, and Norwegian in origin."

Ally asked, "Do you mean, like, Vikings?"

Professor McAdams smiled at her and answered, "Precisely! Daniel and I have been working for years mapping out ancient Mesoamerican cultural sites that strongly suggest Scandinavian explorers managed to work their way along the North American continent, most likely up the Mississippi River, and perhaps even into this area hundreds of years predating the Spanish and French explorers. Our hypothesis works around a sudden unexplainable transition from copper and flint artifacts to mining iron and silver in southeast Missouri, around late 995 to 1000 CE.

"One of the largest Cahokian cities was east of modern-day St. Louis and had at its peak probably ten thousand inhabitants but we could never make a direct connection to Scandinavian culture. However, this lovely little stone is not only Norwegian but were runes and igneous rock commonly used by the late Haakon Sigurdsson, or Haakon the Great."

"Who?" asked JJ, as the other teens looked on with equal confusion etched across their faces.

"Sorry," Professor McAdams replied. "The Christianization of Scandinavian cultures occurred over several hundred years and, at times, was horrifically brutal with conversion often at sword point or worse. One of the jarls, or *earl* in English, was Haakon. He was an ardent defender of the paganism in Norway during this time. A real 'Old Blood' leader who bragged of linage going back to the Norse pagan deity, Odin himself. Scandinavian writings suggest at the peak of his power, Haakon had attracted many ardent followers who were equally opposed to Christianity and aligned with the house of Hladir, essentially his tribe of people, devoted to the old pagan ways.

"To blunt the Christian advances, they reinforced their beliefs through 'Blots' or blood sacrifice. Haakon was successful for many years but eventually fell out of favor, as Christianity's influence grew more dominant and he was supposedly betrayed and murdered.

"One of his most loyal followers, however, was a warrior named Erik Flett, or 'Blood Eagle' as he would later become known. After Haakon was betrayed and murdered, Flett blamed the Christians, pulled together about two dozen ardent followers, and set sail beyond Iceland to never be seen in Europe again. Flett believed if he was truly devoted to the Old Blood, or Odin, in death he would become an Einherjar, which translates loosely, 'Those that fight alone,' or basically an elite Valhalla warrior.

"Along the way, they carved a violent and bloody path through any town or village that had converted to Christianity, where he earned his nickname by ripping out victims' lungs, cutting off their ribs, and spreading their split skin outward like wings, leaving them staked out for all to witness; essentially mocking Christians and their belief in angels and crucifixion. At every blot, Blood Eagle left a trail of vengeance stones behind or runic sigils as a tribute to his former mentor, Haakon. They essentially became his own personal Viking talisman of the day.

"The literature also tells us Blood Eagle encountered another kinsman, Erik Thorvaldsson or Erik the Red, another Old Blood warrior, and stayed with him briefly in Iceland. While Erik the Red was a devout pagan, his wife, and eventually his children, converted to Christianity which no doubt fueled tensions in Iceland.

"Thus, Flett and his followers moved on to 'Vineland' or modern-day St. Johns, a distant Viking outpost at the time founded by Erik the Red. Unfortunately, Erik the Red's most famous son, Leif Erickson, would lead later settlements to Vineland after his father died mysteriously of a plague which he blamed on Flett and his pagan beliefs. In the end, it forced Blood Eagle farther south into the unexplored North American continent and far beyond the reach of Christians or possible retribution.

"The last traces of Flett were left on a Jelling Stone erected by his followers. Simply put, they were claiming the lands beyond Vinland for Odin. It was also surrounded by an altar, built on the bones of indigenous people unfortunate enough to have crossed his path. The stone swore Flett would return one day and enact a terrible vengeance on anyone that abandoned the Old Blood.

"If Blood Eagle and his followers managed to find their way into this area, they would have surely been seen as deities or perhaps semi-deity beings themselves."

Professor Tombs added, "Our hypothesis may be further supported by the Cahokian belief in a 'falcon warrior or birdman' which is often depicted in drawings or burial mounds throughout Mississippian culture, and might locally be indicative historically of Blood Eagle, who also favored the eagle symbol. It's certainly similar in ancient motifs to a falcon. Kindred spirits due to a common symbology, perhaps?"

Professor Tombs produced another survey map from 1960. "I transferred the coordinates from the 1892 map to this one which shows a church was constructed on the mound in the late 1950s and sometime later abandoned. Unfortunately, it seems the mound is now beneath the present-day lake, which means Augie and I will need to pursue a funding grant to perform some remote seismic, sonar surveys and secure an archeological dive team to find and hopefully excavate it."

Ally asked, "Augie, what you said about Viking culture and the 'Old Blood' beliefs, have you ever heard of something like a curse called 'Deathly Alive'?"

He pondered her question. "Scandinavian culture is chalk full of afterlife beliefs surrounding the dead. Sprits and beasts with supernatural mythologies go way back to the earlies paganistic practices. Vikings were no different and believed in several post-burial beings that we would generally call undead today."

Tracy asked, "Like vampires?"

Professor McAdams replied, "Similar for sure. Vampire lore comes from Eastern Europe, whereas Western European myths generally called them revenants."

Tracy pressed, "So what's the difference? And are they like ghosts or, you know, physical?"

Professor McAdams replied, "Think zombie that can remember its past life, or some parts of it at least, but feeds off the living and may even take revenge on those who betrayed them in actual life. Basically, a spirit that comes back and doesn't fully leave its former body. The nastier ones were called 'draugr.' They are very common in Viking lore and even later in Icelandic writings. Vikings believed the draugr would leave their graves to assault the living out of the need for revenge, anger, or even petty jealously. Also, much like common zombie or vampire myth, it was believed anyone killed by a draugr might become a draugr themselves."

Tracy asked guardedly, "What if the person killed was innocent or kind?"

Professor McAdams replied, "No one really knows for sure, of course, as this is old superstitious lore, but regardless of how they were in life, the literature states a draugr is an angry sprit that cannot leave its body in death. It's basically trapped in a curse of undead purgatory, subject to devolve into a murderous and vengeful creature."

JJ then asked what the other teens were thinking. "So, Augie, does a revenant live in a grave, or coffin, or what?"

He nodded and said, "Kind of... They dwell in their graves, but these are usually a burial mounds or cairns. Not a simple grave but in a place of ritual importance. Literature also says they often guard treasure, likely artifacts important to them in life and placed in the cairn when originally sealed—"

Professor Tombs interrupted, "Well, stimulating conversation for certain, but why all this talk about undead Scandinavian spirits? Unless, the Cahokian and Norse artifacts are linked somehow?" He paused while scrutinizing the teens over his spectacles. "Don't suppose you know their origin, because I thought the other day we were discussing native spirit walking?"

JJ glanced at the girls and shrugged, when Tracy said, "Tell them. Tell them everything."

Ally nodded in agreement.

"Sure thing. But you're going to think we're totally mad," JJ said.

JJ told the professors their tale of events over the past four days. Whenever he missed something, Ally and Tracy were quick to provide further details.

Both men sat patiently and said nothing the entire time, but their body language and surprising silence spoke volumes.

Once JJ had finished, Professor Tombs had removed his spectacles and stroked his chin, deep in thought, while Professor McAdams yielded to his elder mentor, clearly trying to process everything they had heard.

After a few seconds of uncomfortable silence, JJ turned back to Tracy and Ally and said, "See, they do think we're crazy. Shoot, I'm not completely sure if we *are* bonkers."

Professor Tombs patted JJ on his hand kindly. "Young man, every part of human history is full of unexplained mythologies, supernatural events, and creatures. Simply because something hasn't been recently documented, doesn't rule out the possibility of its existence, or some portion of ancient lore having a basis in truth. As for your statement, I've given a lot of exams over the years and heard many creative tales, making me a fair judge of character. No, I don't think any of you are unbalanced, and your demeanor, and that of your friends, is anything but deceitful, but I do think you've stumbled across something remarkable and apparently extremely dangerous."

Professor McAdams added, "Daniel is right. Your description of encounters and interactions are inconsistent with any single mythologic creature from either Scandinavian or Cahokian lore. I mean, some parts are textbook for a draugr encounter, but they are supposed to be physical beings imbued with supernatural abilities. Not a disassociated spirit."

Tracy asked, "Can you explain what you mean by textbook or not?"

Professor McAdams continued, "Well, as I said before, if it were a revenant and more specifically a draugr, it would be an animated corpse that can shapeshift, affect the weather, and are always reeking of decay. So, the smell, what assaulted you at the swimming pool and whatever nearly killed your friend, is textbook lore. Whereas the interactions with the spirit called Madeliene, doesn't entirely mesh that mythology due to the non-physical or ghostly appearances."

Tracy asked, "What about the things she warned us about? The Split Moon and Freed on the Nine? It seemed to make the thing mad and called her that weird name."

"*Gamall Blar*, I think?" Ally added.

"I don't recognize the first two things, but *Gamall Blar* is old Norwegian and, directly translated, means 'Old Blue'; literally, the 'Blood of Immortality.' Remember, the pagan beliefs were all tied into blood rituals and beliefs that immortality arose from ancient bloodlines tracing back to creation and the gods themselves."

Professor Tombs added, "I need to go back to Wash U. and refresh my aging memory. May I take the arrowheads with me? I'd like to compare them directly with other Cahokian artifacts we've uncovered near St. Louis, because something about them is remarkably familiar, but I simply cannot recall what."

The teens all agreed to let him borrow the arrowheads for further study and allowed Dr. McAdams to borrow the runestone. Dr. McAdams, however, agreed to stay in town and work remotely from the library while digging deeper into the draugr lore.

Ally then asked the men what all the teens were thinking. "Augie, what if this thing comes after us again? How can we stop it?"

With a hint of anger, Tracy added, "Or kill it?"

Dr. McAdams replied, "The old Scandinavian legends are mixed, but one thing is consistent: it requires a great hero to take on and survive such a creature which is already dead. And, unfortunately, none of us fit that description. Also, it would take a weapon of mythic properties to even harm one."

Dr. Tombs added supportively, "Our strength, however, is knowledge and understanding, and finding out what we are dealing with first and foremost. Have you told your parents? Especially Ms. Hillman, with your father being the local sheriff? I mean, you've told us how this thing has seriously hurt your friend, attacked you, and apparently even murdered a man in town. Whether he believes you or not, I think he should know."

Tracy nodded in agreement and said she would tell her dad tonight at home.

JJ asked Professor Tombs, "Can I make a copy of the old church survey and river map to show my dad? He spends most of his free time fishing and knows every cove and bend of this lake."

The professor agreed and quickly printed one off for him.

***

Leaving the library, the teens stopped briefly in the parking lot to talk among themselves.

JJ asked, "Tracy, are you really going to tell your dad about this and our day?"

Tracy replied, "I'm going to tell him some of it but leave out missing school today. What about you two—Ally? JJ?"

JJ was first to respond. "Like you, parts, I think. But I really want to know more about the lake, so maybe not much yet. At least until we hear back from the professors."

Ally shook her head from side to side dramatically and said, "Sure. I'm going to tell my Evangelical Christian pastor dad and equally devoted mom that an ancient Viking, undead monster is loose on the town and has trapped the ghost of girl that probably committed suicide in the old church back in 1961. Oh, I certainly can't forget to tell them how it may be living under the foundations of the former church that was burnt to the ground after the last reverend went mental and probably sold his soul." She subsequently laughed sarcastically. "Not going to happen, ever, ever, ever. Unless…I want to be locked up like Madeliene was at home for a long time. I will, however, see if I can find out anything more tonight from Dad and let's meet up tomorrow again at school."

As the girls drove home, they passed Mr. Jay's home which was a flurry of local and county police. The yard and home were roped off with yellow caution tape and both police and several detectives were there, as well as Tracy's dad and Deputy Talon who were talking at the end of the driveway.

Her dad, unfortunately, glanced up before they could pass unnoticed, grimaced, and then waved at them to stop. "Ben, would you please let Ally sit in your car for a spell. My daughter and I need to have private conversation."

Ally, nodded without protest, turned back to Tracy with an eyeroll, and stepped out and back into the deputy's car.

"Mind explaining to me what you, Ally, and a boy matching JJ's description were doing in Warsaw today during school hours?" her dad asked. It was a familiar tone that said he was anything but happy with her. "And before you BS me, be aware Mike already called and said you were asking about Mrs. Cross, and spotted the three of you outside in my SUV which you happen to be driving today."

"Something bad killed Mrs. Cross," Tracy said nervously.

To which her dad corrected, "You mean *someone*."

"No, Dad, I mean *something*," she replied more firmly while watching for Ally's reaction in the deputy's car, who was nodding and mouthing: *Tell them.*

"The thing that killed Mrs. Cross attacked Tommy the other night. It also killed Mr. Jay last night."

Her dad sighed deeply in frustration, shifted his weight, and said, "Kiddo, Tommy was hurt by a freak storm. Nothing more. As for Mrs. Cross and Mr. Jay, well that's entirely different and we're still investigating their deaths. I know you're upset about Tommy. Can't blame you at all, but you know how intense your mom is about these things. When she finds out you ditched school today, especially with your friends, well, Tracy Joe Hillman, your free time is going to be seriously curtailed."

"Dad," she protested loudly, "Tommy told me it was a *thing* that attacked him in the storm! He told me so! And Uncle Mike told me about the death of Mrs. Cross and her bruises. I know it killed Mr. Jay because…" she paused, too afraid to say it out loud.

"How do you know this?" he asked, concerned. "If you know something I don't, you need to speak up right now? Because we probably have a psycho on the loose in this town."

"Because it came after me too! At the pool yesterday," she replied, tears welling in her eyes while raising her sweatshirt to reveal the dark bruises. "It wasn't a man; it was something unnatural."

Expecting an explosion, her dad unpredictably grabbed Tracy, hugged her tightly, then said firmly but lovingly, "Stay put." He barked at his deputy, "Ben, call the high school security, shut down the school grounds and pool! Then tag Pete from the detective team for backup, take one of the techs and get over there and process the area for anything."

The deputy nodded obediently and called the school while gathering the others.

The sheriff walked back up the driveway and eventually returned with Deputy Christine Baker. "Kiddo, you know Deputy Baker. She's going to follow you girls home, take your statements, and photograph your bruises."

Tracy asked, "So you're not mad at me?"

He replied, "Frustrated, yeah, kiddo! You really should have told me this yesterday right after you were assaulted." He sighed. "But I get it. Things are crazy right now."

Ally, who had gotten out of the deputy's car, asked, "You believe us, Sheriff?"

"Miss Denton, I believe someone very sick is harming people around here, and after what I saw inside Mrs. Cross's, and now Mr. Jay's house, I'm open to almost anything."

After Deputy Baker departed, following his daughter and friend home, Deputy Talon stopped before leaving for the high school and asked, "You don't really think something supernatural is loose, do you, Sheriff?"

He shook his head and replied, "Ben, you and I are both military and law enforcement vets. We've seen a lot of horrible things in our day, but what happened to Mr. Jay...well, I have no idea what could possibly pick up a 150-pound man and pin him helplessly to a wall, while ripping out his lungs, ribs, and filleting him like a sick angel. Do you?"

The deputy shook his head. "Maybe it's a group of perps, you know, like a devil-worshiping cult?"

"Yeah, maybe. But then what killed his birds without leaving a mark on them? It just doesn't add up. Anyway, 've got to call my wife and finish up here and then check in with Mayor Thornton. No, I don't think we're ready to announce to her or the press that a monster is rampaging in River Rock." The sheriff removed his hat, ran his fingers through his hair in frustration, then said, "Just get on over to the school."

Deputy Talon obediently replied, "Rodger that, Sheriff."

As he was walking away, the sheriff added, "Watch your darn six, Ben! At least until we know what the heck is going on around here. And, if anything, and I do mean anything, seems weird, call in for backup. No heroics today."

Later that evening, Ally called JJ.

"Can you talk?"

JJ replied, "Yes, I'm in my room. What's going on?"

"Tracy's dad saw us on the way home. We drove past Mr. Jay's house, but that was a mistake. Her mom knows and flipped completely out. She naturally called my mom. So, we are both in lockdown—can't leave. And I heard school is being cancelled tomorrow due to the police processing the pool. Did you talk to your dad yet?"

"Yes. I told him some professors from Wash U. were in town researching old Native American sites and mentioned a possible location. When I showed him the map, he said that place is where the old church sat and wasn't a spot most anglers visited, because fish didn't bite there, and it was dicey getting a boat in and out without snagging things. He tried it himself a few times over the years but was never able to catch anything there. Dad also said the foundations of the old church are usually underwater, but this year has been a drought, so it wouldn't surprise him if some parts of it are near the surface or even visible, if they haven't rotted completely away."

"So maybe that explains why we're suddenly seeing the draugr?" Ally asked. "Madeliene told us water was its weakness, but with the lake level down, maybe that's how it got loose after decades trapped underwater?"

He replied, "I was thinking the same thing. I've also been thinking about Madeliene's warnings and searching for anything I can find on draugr lore online. She said three things to us about a Split Moon, freed on the nine, and Gamall Blar. We know from Augie the last thing, but the others didn't make sense."

"Did you find anything?" she asked.

"Sort of. Seems the old pagan and Norse literature are full of references to the numbers three, nine, and the lunar phases. The number nine was common in Viking writings surrounding the undead. The Split Moon reference, however, was not clear, but it started me thinking, what if it means half-moon? So, I referenced the lunar phases for this week."

"You're killing me, JJ. What did you find?"

"Mrs. Cross was killed on Friday, April 1st during the New Moon lunar phase, or let's call it: day one. On Sunday, two days later, Madeliene appears with whatever is stalking her, or day three. We had another contact with her today, or almost on day six that starts tomorrow, a multiple of three. In three more days, it will be Saturday, April 9th and first quarter lunar phase, or maybe a Split Moon? Ally, there is a pattern here and everything is somehow weirdly connected but also getting scary."

"Wow, I would have never put those pieces together so fast, but it makes total sense. Your brain always sees patterns the rest of us can't."

"That's not all. Madeliene's name has nine letters. Could be coincidence, but considering the past week, I'm not so sure. She also died October 28th and, according to Reverend Rite, was violated on October 31st and rose a couple nights after. So, I checked and the lunar cycle for quarter moon peaked on October 31st that year, also it's a big pagan holiday. Not specifically Norse, but a big deal in a lot of pagan literature. Lastly, April 9th is, get this, a holiday in Norway that celebrates the life of...Drum roll, please...Haakon Sigurdsson."

"Wait. That's the guy Blood Eagle followed, right?" Ally replied, shocked.

"Yes. Erik Flett. The same last name as Madeliene's mother, who was also Norwegian. Ally, these many things lining up are statistically impossible to be coincidence. I think something is building up to happen this Friday or Saturday, and whatever occurs will be awful, but there seems to be a missing piece somewhere that ties it all together."

"Tell me you're not thinking about going out there. Because it's way too dangerous!"

"My dad said I could borrow his boat, and I called Augie and suggested a reconnaissance trip tomorrow morning or the next day. Besides, I suspect your dad is going to work his way back around to my parents soon, and then I'll be on lockdown, no doubt. So, if there is something that can help us, we need to act quickly."

"What if it's there, JJ? Madeliene said she feared the Rev. Can't you see? Not the reverend, as Tracy said, but the *revenant*."

"I thought of that too. But we still need to see if we can see parts of the old church or find anything useful. Plan is to stay on the water and firmly in the boat. She said it hated water. Also, read online that draugr, like many undead, have a strong dislike for iron. Won't kill it, but should at least repel it. So, I'm also taking along my granddad's old shotgun. He hand-packed his old shells with iron shot."

"I'm glad at least the professor is going too but it's still very risky. Also, you can't kill it anyway, 'cause it's already dead, you dork."

"Ha, right you are, Ally." He laughed lightly. "Don't worry, I'll be careful."

"I wish Tracy and I could go with you. Call me right after you get back 'cause I want to know everything."

JJ said, "Here, I'm sending you and Tracy permission to track my cellphone, that way you can see where we are tomorrow. You and Tracy need to do it too, at least until this nightmare is over. Meanwhile, what are you doing tomorrow?"

"Oh, I'll be at church all day with Mom and Dad," she replied flatly. "They aren't letting me out of their sight for a long while." She sighed. "Surprised they didn't take my cellphone. Tracy's mom has her on a short leash too, but at least she's going over to Clinton to spend the day with Tommy."

"Ally, I'm going to crash. Got an early morning."

"Me too, JJ. Right after I journal and then turn in. Be careful, you dork."

Chapter 6 – A Broken Sigil

Tracy awoke to the sound of a church organ. It was playing "Ave Maria" which made her shiver after the events from Madeliene's home the day before. Looking around, as tendrils of sleep cleared her vision, Tracy realized she was not at home in bed but instead sitting in an old wooden pew, inside a small country church. Standing up, she was immediately greeted by a familiar and equally surprised voice:

"Tracy?"

Turning around, Ally and JJ were both there as well.

"Tracy... You're both here too, but how?" asked Ally.

Tracy, equally confused, added, "But where are we?"

Her question was replied to by a different but familiar voice, "It is a memory."

The teens turned around and there was Madeliene. But she was solid, not ghostly, and her dress was crisp and clean white, not faded or soiled with time. And there was no gaping wound on her neck, nor any indication of death.

She appeared normal, like any other teen. Madeliene said, "I brought you back into my last memory before the revenant turned me. It's the last piece of my life he cannot corrupt or see. Here we are safe to talk without fear or intrusion."

"Where's Tommy?" Tracy asked, concerned.

She smiled at Tracy and extended her hand, as a dear friend would. Tracy grasped her hand without hesitation, amazed it wasn't cold or painful to the touch.

"Your Tommy has not fully recovered, and I dare not risk bringing him here. He is a champion, which is why it probably attacked him first. It will also be watching him closely, but he is safe for now. I keep causing as much trouble as possible to shift its attention," she added with mischievous grin.

Madeliene led them out of the church and into the field outside. She pointed to a place under the backside of the church's foundation and said, "The entrance is in there. But do not venture inside for any reason. He is all powerful within that place and never alone. There are others bound to him since the time of his death."

"Others like him and how many?" asked JJ.

"Twenty-six and with him, makes one more. They are his to command, but for now at least, their souls are tied to his lair and cannot venture beyond."

"Another multiple of nine," to which Madeliene nodded in agreement. "Is that what drew him to you?" JJ asked.

"My family lineage is tied to him and as my mother was fond of saying, I was cursed by the Old Blood."

"What exactly does that mean?" Ally asked.

"I was born with a blood deficiency. My body did not produce enough red blood which made me severely anemic and, at times, weak. The local doctor used to joke with me as a child that I was a blueblood and thus destined for royalty. It always made me smile, but it made my mother fearful... Well, that and my visions."

Ally probed, "Visions of things to come?"

"Sometimes, but not always," Madeleine replied. "They started soon after my first words. Occasionally, glimpses of things from the past before I was even born. Other times, things yet to occur. They were always bits and pieces, though, and I had no control over them. The visions would come to me without warning, and whenever I told my mother, well...it scared her, so I kept them to myself. But maybe that is why it singled me out? The visions? That spring day at the church, it called out to me and drew me into its lair. Appearing to me disguised as a cat, but I could sense the veil of darkness around it. The creature offered me an escape from my pain, but I knew somehow it was lying."

"The lair entrance was inside a buried mound, lined with three rings of arrowheads, all pointing inward like daggers and nine strange stones spaced out around it, rimmed with glowing blue moss—fairy fire. Terrified, I grabbed one of the stones with my right hand and three of the arrowheads with my left and crawled back out as fast as I could. I hoped it would seal it within."

"But I was wrong because the binding knot above the doorway was already severed. That allowed it to roam beyond its prison. However, the creature has limits, at least for now. I remember its anger searing into me in my wake. At home, later that night, I slipped out of the house, while Mother was resting and into the garden to hide the items under the stones and near the gnomes she had placed outside." Madeliene smiled at that thought, and said with light laugh, "Mother was right that time. He really hates them because they ward him out somehow. My treasures were safe there because he could not reach them. I do not know if the arrowheads matter anymore, but he needs all nine of the stones."

JJ smacked himself in the head. "Except I removed them, ah, I'm so stupid."

Madeliene said, "I told you to, silly. With mother's passing, they were vulnerable to theft. And now with Reverend Rite's demise, it will simply find and corrupt another to retrieve them, if it hasn't already. The revenant has an uncanny ability to manipulate the weak or as in my case emotionally unstable."

JJ said, "But Reverend Rite is still alive. We saw him earlier today."

"I know, I saw it briefly from his television while searching for you. I should not have lingered, but seeing him again made me so angry. It was a mistake, and once again, I let my emotions take over and betrayed his location. You can be certain Josiah Rite is forever gone from this world."

"Do you remember dying?" Tracy asked.

"Yes, I do. It really hurt," she said, rubbing her chest instinctually. "The last night is still vividly etched in my soul. I knew from my visions it was coming for me. In defense, I wrote down as much as my body would allow and hid my journal where I hoped someone would one day find it. On the way back inside, I remember seeing the Split Moon above me, not directly in the sky, but in my last living vision and then, my heart stopped. Everything seemed to freeze in time, and then…emptiness." Her voice became tinged with sadness. "No light. No angels. Only darkness.

"Then I rose. First confused and filled with overwhelming rage. So angry. I almost killed my mother and the reverend that very night, but the horrific expressions on their faces was enough to bring back my focus. I'm ashamed to say, I spent the next two years tormenting them... I was unbalanced at first. It drove Mother into near isolation and the reverend eventually out of town but that also was to safeguard my treasures.

"Don't feel too sorry for him. He sold you out to that thing," Tracy said consolingly.

"I know. But he also unwittingly did me a favor. When he burned the church down, which I suggested, it closed the entrance locking the creature back inside. It didn't completely free me from his binding, but it did allow me some distance with time to reflect and learn how to better focus my new abilities. Then arrived that glorious lake and I could almost sever the binding on me." Madeliene paused while casting her gaze towards the ground.

"But?" Ally asked.

"To what purpose?" she replied. "I was snared by a revenant, due to my stupid, childish anger and jealously over what other kids in my time had and I did not. Now look at me. I'm simply a memory or worse, something vile and wicked. Not even worthy of God's gaze."

Tracy squeezed Madeliene's hand and said firmly, "You are not wicked! Otherwise, you wouldn't have saved me or my Tommy. I don't care what your mother told you."

Madeliene smiled at her. "I am sorry if I hurt your arm, but it was the only way to get you in the water." She let go of Tracy's hand, turned away briefly, and sighed. "If I only had such friendship in life, maybe things would have been different." Shaking off her melancholy, Madeliene said firmly, "No matter. I had decades to dwell upon the creature and what it wants. It has also unknowingly betrayed parts of its plan in my visions which have become stronger with the revenant's escape following the recent new moon."

JJ asked, "It's going to get stronger and peak under the Split Moon on Saturday—ah, April 9th? Isn't it?"

"Yes, I knew you would put the pieces together. But it needs an artifact from his time. Something he tricked the local people into making for him from pure iron and silver. He was corrupting it with his vile, dark knowledge of the old ones when his plan was discovered and they locked him away. I don't know what the artifact was, but I've seen the nine binding runestones in my vision. If he can gather all the pieces together, and somehow me, he will forge a weapon that permanently frees him of his bindings; forever immortal and invincible. Worse, he will rupture the lair, raise his followers, and any that falls beneath his weapon thereafter while exerting a bloody revenge back to his homeland."

"Any chance you know where the artifact is located?" JJ asked.

"I caught a glimpse of it once, a piece I was able to pick unwillingly from a dark thought. It lies in a place where many people once worshiped, long ago. High on a grassy mound surrounded by others, some larger, some smaller. In a place where it was forged but ultimately cursed. So dark, where many were buried but not completely dead." Madeleine, held her hands to her eyes, voice wavering with dread. "In my vision, I can hear their screams—hands outstretched, upward, pleading as the dirt was pushed in around them, suffocating, the muffled cries for mercy fading away one by one, replaced by cruel silence. It too is marked by the nine, but I do not know what any of that vision means because it was his. And worse, it brought him pleasure."

Madeliene sat down cross-legged on the floor, eyes again cast downward and began to lightly weep.

Tracy sat down beside her and cradled Madeliene. "We will figure it out. Like I said before, we will save you. I promise."

Madeliene stared at Tracy, JJ, and Ally. "This was the last memory that belonged only to me. It was the one place I could go and rest without enduring pain. Listen to my favorite song and dream. I'm glad I could share it with all of you." Her face contorted in slight pain as she said, "His memory has now invaded mine, so it is no longer safe here anymore. We must stop him at all costs. I know, but then if we succeed, what am I to become? I am a revenant and fear being doomed to a never ending, vile, existence. I understand now and fear the Deathly Alive and want for nothing but to go home."

The sadness in her voice even made JJ tear up.

Tracy hugged her tightly and said, "We will figure it all out and find a way to help you too. I promise."

Madeliene stopped weeping, gazed into the distance, and said, "My memory is almost spent." She turned her head sideways, as if listening to someone in the distance. "He's found another living servant to do his bidding. To obtain the artifact." Madeliene held her hands to her temples, eyes closed tightly, intense with concentration. "I can't see him...yet. Too many shadows and dark thoughts. Be careful...NO!" she suddenly screamed while rising to her feet.

"What is it?" Tracy exclaimed.

Madeliene replied, "He's after Tommy! It still believes he is your champion. You must stop him and go now!

Panicking, Tracy screamed, "WHAT CAN WE DO?"

As the memory began to crumble like a dream where everyone was breaking apart. But they all heard Madeliene's voice fading away, along with their last tendrils of sleep.

"GNOMES!"

It was after four a.m. when Tracy woke and began screaming, exactly when the lights turned on in Ally's house next-door.

Tracy was pleading with her dad, "IT'S GOING TO KILL TOMMY! PLEASE! WE'VE GOT TO GET TO THE HOSPITAL NOW!"

Sheriff Hillman was still wiping the sleep from his eyes along with his wife, both equally shaken from their sleep. He figured his daughter's sudden emotional trauma was only a bad dream, until Ally appeared pounding at their door.

"SHERIFF! IT'S AFTER TOMMY!"

Shaking off his grogginess, and with Ally's parents showing up on his doorstep behind their daughter, he tried to make sense of what exactly was going on. In all the confusion, the sheriff finally barked firmly at Ally, "Ms. Denton, stay put with your parents! Tracy, get in my car!" He grabbed his go-bag and duty belt on the way out the door, and they jumped in.

As the sheriff's car pulled away from the house, lights on and siren wailing, he was already on his radio calling dispatch. "Dispatch! Call the Henry County Sheriff's Office and have them get a patrol over to the hospital, ASAP! Hell, send two. Someone is after the Baskin's kid. And call Ben, he lives near Clinton and have him meet me at the emergency entrance."

Tracy pressed, "Faster, Dad, please!"

Her dad grumbled. "You better be right about this, kiddo. Now, hang on."

The car sped off towards the hospital.

Pulling into the parking lot and squealing up to the emergency entrance, Deputy Talon was already there and jumped out of his car to greet them.

The sheriff asked him urgently, "Henry, county here?"

"Sheriff, it's alright. Henry and Clinton both sent a unit. I checked in with them few minutes ago when I rolled up. Tommy Baskins is fine. The nurse woke him, checked his vitals, and is probably resting."

Tracy protested, "Dad, we need to get up there now. It's coming for him!"

Deputy Talon said, "Tracy, there are four uniforms by or in his room. I can assure you, no one is getting near Tommy."

Sheriff Hillman drew a deep breath, almost a sigh of relief. "Well, kiddo, we're here. Let's at least check in on him."

They all walked into the hospital, found the elevators, and went up to critical care, second floor, and Tommy's room. The sheriff stopped in the hallway to talk with the two Clinton and Henry County officers while Tracy slipped quietly into Tommy's room, who was awake and smiled.

"Hey, you."

"Hey, you," she replied sweetly.

"I know I'm popular and all, but what's going on, Tee?"

"Madeliene warned me to come here."

"Funny you mentioned her. Because I could have sworn I saw her reflection in the tube right before all the uniforms showed up. But thought I was dreaming."

As if on cue, the winds suddenly blew intensely and the clouds outside rolled, causing the hair on their arms to rise.

Tommy said, "Holy crap on a cracker, it's back!"

Outside the hospital, it was like the entire sky erupted as a force veiled in darkness blew in through the large plate-glass windows at the opposite end of the hall, showering fragments everywhere, and shutting off the electricity, including the backup generator. The impact sent staff screaming, flying, or ducking behind their desks or into adjacent rooms for cover; some injured by the assorted debris. The impact also sent a shockwave rippling down the hallway and knocked all six of the officers to the ground.

Shaken but defiant, Sheriff Hillman stood back up, along with the other officers. The entire wall and windows at the end of the hallway had been blown wide open and was now filled with a dark, rolling cloud churning with an unseen presence that set all their nerves on edge. Worse was an overwhelming smell of pure death.

Sheriff Hillman barked, "BEN, GET IN THERE AND PROTECT MY LITTLE GIRL AND TOMMY!" while officers drew their service revolvers and stood fast.

Deputy Talon dashed back into Tommy's room, standing in a defensive position and immediately behind the door.

Inside the room, Tracy, who was kneeling beside Tommy's bed, said frantically, "IS ANYTHING IN THIS ROOM MADE OF IRON?"

Deputy Talon asked, "What...What do you mean?"

Tracy replied, "ONLY IRON CAN HURT IT!"

Meanwhile, the force outside roared out a deafening sound of a large bull that churned and barreled down the hallway.

From Tommy's room, they heard the officers' guns firing dozens of rounds, a crashing, screams of the men, and other horrific sounds followed only by an abrupt and absolute silence.

The door handle turned slowly and stopped, locked by the deputy. Another brief silence, followed by a sound Deputy Talon would never forget as the heavy wooden door peeled aside, like piece of tissue paper, leaving him the only person standing between Tommy and Tracy and staring at something surely straight out of the pit of Hell.

As the force surged towards him, it shimmered once again into a towering man-like shape. Deputy Talon snapped out his baton and swung with everything he had. It was the only iron in the room.

The thing painfully recoiled, swirled, and retorted with an unexpected tone of excitement, "Einherjar, Einherjar! Finally, after so many years, something worthy to kill."

It lunged at him again, and the deputy responded with another blow from his baton, this time with Tracy hurling a pitcher of water from Tommy's bedside.

When the water and iron baton hit the force, it shuttered and roared, "Ah, you've been talking to the little witch!" It shifted back into a writhing, skinless, black bull eyes, dark and lifeless that nearly filled the hallway beyond the shattered doorframe.

The revenant roared its unholy sound, stomped its mighty cloven hooves, shattering tile floors with immense arcane power.

But before it could strike, JJ appeared, sliding narrowly by it on the floor between the creature and the deputy. Flipping over in mid-slide, he slammed a small garden gnome in front of him while pulling out his grandpa's sawed-off shotgun, and yelled, "CHEW ON THIS YOU OVERSIZED TURD!" He fired both barrels, point blank, releasing twelve-gauge, double-aught, iron shot.

The force squealed in an unholy and confused rage before whirling away, ripping back down the hallway, and in its path stripping the walls with sprays of blue lighting and fury before erupting back out through the opening it made, disappearing into the misty darkness eastward.

As JJ sat up, Deputy Talon moved over to him. "Are you, hurt?" He quickly checked JJ over for any injuries.

Shaking as his adrenaline was rapidly wearing off, JJ replied, "No, sir...but I think I'll sit here for a few minutes, if it's alright with you." He slid over to lean back against Tommy's bed while the deputy pulled the shotgun away from his shaking fingers.

Tracy, meanwhile, dashed past them both into the hall and screamed for help, which sent the deputy running into the chaotic emergency and what was left the second floor of the building.

The teens sat in silence for several minutes while emergency and hospital staff moved frantically to attend to the wounded officers, Sheriff Hillman, their own staff, and some patients throughout the floor.

Tracy slipped back in and said, "Dad and the other officers are going down to emergency. They're all...I've got to get down there and call my mom!"

Tommy replied, "Go on, Tee. We're good here."

She quickly kissed Tommy on lips and JJ on top of his head before dashing back into the hall and the emergency room downstairs.

Tommy tapped his friend on the shoulder and said flatly, "JJ."

"Yeah?"

"Dude, that was, like, the coolest thing I've ever seen! Hell, you even called it a turd!" This made them both chuckle.

"Want to know a secret?" JJ asked sheepishly.

"You bet," Tommy replied.

JJ lowered his gaze to his shoes, and embarrassed said, "We are so in over our heads." He was now shaking all over.

Tommy rolled over and flicked the back of JJ's ear, the way he had when they were kids trying to annoy each other; it caused JJ to flinch.

"Tommy, what the hell?" he asked while rubbing his ear.

"I'm stuck here. Tee must deal with her dad, and Ally is in lockdown. So, what are you doing sitting down? Get your rear-end up and get out of here."

"Are you deaf? Deputy Talon told me to stay put," JJ replied.

"Tee said something bad is going to happen soon, in like two or three days, right? Well, the way I figure, by the time this mess gets sorted out, the dead Viking dude's got the upper hand. Go find the professor at the library and put that super brain of yours to work. Maybe Madeliene can help in some way."

"Tommy, it's not like I can call her, you know."

He smiled at JJ. "Dude, for someone so smart, you are dumb. Have you ever tried?"

JJ nodded. "Lightbulb, Tommy. You're brilliant!" He smacked his head in acknowledgement. "I can't exactly walk out of here, though." JJ pointed to the chaos in the hallway.

"Leave that to me," Tommy said, holding up his nurse call remote and squeezing it "AGGGH!" he yelled as loud as he could and kept yelling in fainted agony.

Both the deputy and a nurse responded. While busy with Tommy, they failed to notice JJ slipping quietly away.

The remainder of the hospital was equally chaotic, giving JJ easy access to the stairway, hospital exit and his car without even being noticed. He started the car and drove back to River Rock, as fast as his dad's old El Camino would go.

In route, he tried calling out Madeliene's name several times, but nothing happened. Shaking his head in frustration, he grabbed his cellphone and punched in Professor McAdam's number.

"Mr. Duncan?" answered the professor.

"Professor...Augie, this is JJ. Can you meet me at the Long Shoals Marina?"

"Are you alright? The news said there was an explosion at the Clinton Hospital. Isn't your friend there?"

"Tommy's fine. Thanks. But, sir, it's getting stronger and I have a bad feeling we need to get out on the river to figure out what this thing wants. It's missing something, and if we don't figure it out soon, I don't think anything can stop it."

After a brief pause, he replied, "Alright, JJ. I'll meet you at the marina by the boat launch. Is there anything I can bring?"

"Some iron would be nice. And whatever you do, don't bring the stone with you."

Chapter 7 – Cairn of Souls

After an hour of lecture from Ally's dad and mom, and over an hour of prayer for the hysterical awakening, they drove her to their church after breakfast to spend the rest of the day. It was past 8:30 a.m. when she slipped into the bathroom to briefly escape her parents and into a stall and pulled out her cellphone. Tapping on the tracker app, she saw Tracy and Tommy were both in Clinton, still at the hospital. However, Tommy, to her dismay, was on Truman Lake.

She texted him: *Are you seriously going where I think you're going?!!*

The text said, "read," and after a brief "..." replied: *Three-hour tour...I hope but have Augie with me.*

Ally started to reply but was interrupted by her mother's voice:

"Are you alright in there, Ally?"

"Going to the bathroom, Mom. I'm fine," she replied tersely.

Text me when you get back!!! she typed to JJ.

Once the message showed as "read," she flushed the toilet to bluff her mom, stuffed her cellphone back into her pocket, and washed up at the sink before exiting the bathroom to find her mom waiting outside.

"Ally, your father needs some help in the sanctuary. Please get in there while I help prepare a few lunches for the afternoon youth group."

Ally obediently nodded and, on the way into the sanctuary, knelt briefly and said a silent prayer for JJ's safe return. Afterward, she found her dad at the pulpit drafting his next sermon.

He glanced up from his notes as she entered the chapel and said, "Excellent. You are exactly the person I was hoping to see. I need a second opinion from someone your age. You know how to reach out to our youth group and not appear too lame."

She approached her dad and, without prompting, hugged him tightly.

He lightly chuckled while hugging her back. "What brought this on?"

She replied, "I don't know, Daddy. I just wanted to show you how much I love you."

He smiled and replied, "Well, God does work in mysterious ways. I may have to rethink my sermon."

"I need to work on some homework. Can I please use your office?"

"Sure, Ally. I'll check on your mom. If it's for school, you're welcome to use my laptop."

"Thanks, Daddy."

She left the sanctuary and strode down the hall to his office, closed the door, once behind his desk, pulled out the envelopes of photographs and letters they had retrieved from Mrs. Cross's home, and began to read.

***

JJ, meanwhile, was navigating his dad's old pontoon boat to the shallows on a branch of Truman Lake and nearing the location of the former Old Town and church. It normally was a dicey area full of submerged timber and brush, but things had been made worse today by the overcast sky and persistent mist. Even worse, the banks of the lake were clouded in a thick, unyielding fog. Fortunately, his dad's boat was equipped with a trolling motor and visual sonar depth and fish-finder to help them slowly navigate snags and keep from running aground. JJ operated the boat while Augie stayed on the bow, armed with a snagging pole, to watch for anything sticking out or any large driftwood that might damage their craft.

In route, Augie asked if he or any of the others had learned anything new since they last talked at the library.

JJ relayed their encounter at the Cross's house, at least most of it, and about their "dream" meeting with Madeliene. When he discussed what she had said about the vile vision of people being buried alive, and something to do with the nine, Augie's face noticeably lit up.

"Did I say something useful?" he asked the professor.

Augie nodded. "Yes. I think so. Your description of Madeliene's vision sounds terrifyingly familiar. The Cahokian Mounds Daniel discussed before by St. Louis has a structure that has always been a bit of a mystery since it was first excavated. Back then, Daniel was working on his undergrad and graduate degrees in the late sixties and early seventies. He wrote several publications about it: how native religious beliefs seem to loosely intertwine with old European mythologies. I helped Daniel and the park service work on it some during my graduate years but, unfortunately, didn't really contribute anything significant. Not like Daniel, at any rate. It's known today as 'Mound Number Seventy-Two,' but it always left me with an unsettling feeling to work around."

The professor shook his head uncomfortably and said, "We can discuss more later, best to keep our wits about us, because I can barely see the water in this fog."

The weather conditions were far less than ideal, but after two hours, JJ had gradually steered the boat into the location of the former church. Exactly as his dad had predicted, and due to the winter drought, most of the old mound and ruins were exposed above the waterline and perched like a small island sticking out in the lake and near the southern bank.

While the thick fog made any structure details impossible to see, it's submerged outline was easily mapped by the sonar and data-trip logger. After making a pass around the mound, but keeping hopefully a safe distance away, Augie asked JJ to hold the boat still so he also could review the trip log. JJ brought the boat to a stop and quietly slid their anchor into the water, allowing the professor to leave the bow and begin pouring over the captured data.

"This is odd," he said.

"What is it?" JJ asked.

The professor pointed to the screen and replied, "The shape. It's not oval or round like traditional mounds we've uncovered at other Mesoamerican sites. It's more like... Oh, my God. It's shaped like a bootheel." He started to chuckle lightly. Seeing the confused expression on JJ's face, the professor patted him on the shoulder. "Not a simple mound or cairn, but like Sutton Hoo or an old Anglo-Saxon burial mound. Don't you see? The cairn was built over their ship! I think we just stumbled upon definitive proof that Vikings were here, hundreds of years before the Spanish! I'll be darned, Daniel was right and is going to totally flip out!"

In all the professor's excitement, they hadn't noticed a sudden drop in temperature until both began to shiver. JJ, seeing Augie's breath and then his own, turned towards the mound and spotted something moving in the fog onshore. He leapt up to the bow and weighed anchor while Augie grabbed his pole, when the professor noticed something floating by their boat.

With JJ back behind the trolling motor, the professor probed at something in the water and retrieved a dead crow, and then spotted another and yet another, and recited out loud, "Fowl will drop dead if passing over a cairn or barrow...I think it would be best to reverse course, JJ, and get away from here."

"On it, Augie," JJ replied who had already begun turning the pontoon around to depart when it struck something solid and stopped moving.

According to their sonar, however, there was nothing that should have stopped the boat. But then arose that vile smell, and JJ knew all too well, while tendrils of light started rolling off the island, underwater, and crackled with that familiar blueish glow he had seen in Mrs. Cross's garden and hospital.

Augie yelled, "Foxfire, by God, it's coming!" and retrieved two iron rods from his backpack, tossing one to JJ.

Their boat twisted and turned roughly in the water as it began to drift back towards the mound. Then multiple shadowy, skeletal figures rose out of the churning water and grabbing at the pontoon rails to pull themselves aboard; each with the reek of decay, dark, eyeless skulls locked forever in a lifeless grin from beneath their rusted helms.

JJ and Augie struck the boarding figures, one after another with the iron rods, but as fast as they could dislodge one, it was replaced by another. Clearly, dozens had surrounded their boat and, despite their best efforts, they were trapped and being overwhelmed.

After almost a minute of fighting off the undead host, their boat was less than ten feet from shore and barely within two feet of water where the fog had thinned, and they could see it. A towering warrior, clad in corroded armor, and wearing a helmet adorned with wings of silver. Red Eagle was a menacing figure, necrotic-black with foxfire rippling from its outstretched axe, dripping with visceral pieces of flesh and fresh blood.

"GIVE ME MY STONE!"

Its voice boomed and sent chills down both JJ and Augie spines.

JJ asked, "Please tell me you didn't bring it with you."

The professor replied, "No, I left it locked in my hotel room safe."

Their boat was almost within reach of the revenant, when a flash of violet lightning crackled above them and danced around the boat, racing along the side rails, and sending the undead host plunging back into the churning water.

JJ, understanding what had happened, jumped back behind the boat's captain chair, grabbed the steering wheel, and punched the throttle forward while yelling, "HANG ON, AUGIE!"

Driving the outboard motor hard, the boat lurched upward and freed itself from the hidden hoard, whooshing back down the old river channel leaving a deep wake behind, as fast as it could carry them away to safety.

In the distance behind, they heard thunderous explosions and saw intense illumination within the fog from visceral exchanges of blueish-foxfire and violent lighting.

Recovering, the professor got back into his seat after rolling to the floor during their escape, sat quietly for a few seconds and subsequently, after taking a deep sigh, "Well, the body of evidence absolutely supports that was a draugr."

JJ replied dryly, "You think so, Professor?"

To which they both laughed in nervous relief.

"And as for the rest?" JJ asked.

Augie sat back in his seat, scratched his head, and replied, "Beats the hell out of me."

Once they were back at the marina boat ramp, they loaded the pontoon boat onto its trailer and pulled it out of the lake. The boat's outside was etched with burn marks and nearly all the rails surrounding the deck were damaged or torn nearly off, and one of the pontoon logs had been dented from beings of superhuman strength.

JJ shook his head and said, "Glad it's a tritoon or we'd might have sunk before getting back." He sighed with exasperation. "If the revenant doesn't kill me, my dad absolutely will once he gets back in town and sees this."

Augie recommended JJ take his boat home and check in with his friends. Meanwhile, he would go back to the hotel, secure the stone, and call Dr. Tombs to give the news of their findings. "I need to get Daniel back in town so we can go over everything we've learned to date and maybe figure out how to stop this thing."

"Do you think we can stop it?" JJ asked. "I mean now that you've seen what it can do."

Augie replied, "Maybe, if we can figure out what it is searching for. We know it needs the last runestone but, like you said, there is still another missing piece to the puzzle. Let's hope Daniel's research can shed light on things I can't, and finally put it all together. And then, we need to speak to the authorities, so none of us gets ourselves killed in the process."

"Can we meet at the library later this evening?" JJ asked.

"Let's plan on first thing tomorrow morning instead because it will take me at least six hours to pick up Daniel from Wash U. and drive back. Despite his positive demeanor, Daniel's health has declined significantly in the past few years, and he cannot see well enough to drive at night either. He will also be tired, but no worries. I know he will want to get back here to go over our findings."

JJ added, "Sorry, I didn't know about Professor Tombs' condition, and I don't want to seem cruel, but we're running out of time. That's all."

Augie replied, "Believe me, I get it. I saw that thing too and I'm still shaking. Let's plan on meeting at eight tomorrow morning, but text me if anything changes, and I will too."

JJ said, "Definitely. Sounds good, Augie."

"Oh, and one other thing, I don't know what to say but for whatever it's worth, please thank your friend for helping us out back there. I'm certain we would have never gotten back without that little light show."

"I will, Professor."

They parted ways and JJ started driving back to his house.

Passing by the town of River Rock along the winding State Highway Seven, things had changed while they were on the lake. There were police everywhere, local and state highway patrol, and National Guard units too.

JJ skipped stopping in town for gas to avoid the roadblocks and drove straight home. Pulling into his family's property, he quietly backed the pontoon behind his dad's workshop, and safely out of direct sight from the house. Walking up to house, he was greeted by his kid sister Lena's annoying voice:

"You're gonna get it."

"Jimmy James Duncan! Where on earth have you been?" His mom greeted him, arms crossed and glaring at him with a mixture of anger and relief.

"Ah, fishing. School was cancelled today," he replied.

"Oh, don't start with me, young man! I've already heard from the sheriff's office this morning. They told me there was an explosion, maybe a gas leak or something, at the hospital before dawn and you were there. It's all over the news too. My God, several people died and Jack Hillman's in critical condition."

"Mom, I'm sorry for not telling you but I had the worst feeling last night. I couldn't sleep and really needed to check on Tommy today, and knew school had been cancelled."

She replied, "It's cancelled for the rest of the week too. Something also happened at the school pool, but no one is really saying anything at this point. I called Sharon Hillman to check on Tommy, and that's when she told me about Tracy and Ally waking them in a panic, then Jack almost getting killed at the hospital. Folks in this town are talking, the news is crazy, and even the weather is a mess. Now there are

National Guard units setting up checkpoints all over town. Something about a maniac on the loose in River Rock, and then you simply up and disappear. Do you have any idea how worried I've been?"

"Sorry, Mom. I should have told you my plans—I needed to clear my head after this morning. But I never meant to worry you."

She calmed, shook her head, and said, "You're lucky your father's on the road until Saturday." She held out her hand. "Cough up the keys."

Knowing exactly what she meant, JJ reached into his pocket and handed her his car keys without protest.

"I will call the sheriff's office back and let them know you're home and safe. And you're not going anywhere until your dad gets back. Understand?"

JJ nodded and replied obediently, "Yes, ma'am."

"Good. Now get cleaned up; you're a mess, and I'll have supper ready in an hour." She abruptly hugged him and added, "Don't you ever worry me like that again, JJ."

JJ did as he was told, but in the bathroom, he texted Ally: *Back home, can we talk later?*

Ally replied a few seconds later: *Call me after ten, when parents will think I'm asleep...K?*

After supper, JJ helped clean up the kitchen, bundled up the trash and took it outside to their can. After placing it in the bin, he reattached the bungie on top that kept the racoons out of their trash. He was about to go inside when he noticed Madeliene over by their outbuilding door, making a motion for him to follow her inside. He held up his hand directing her to stay put and stepped inside the back kitchen door, and called out, "Hey, Mom? I need to go out to the shop and get the trash out before Dad gets back home. Okay?"

"Okay. But then straight back inside because it's getting dark."

JJ sprinted across the lightly foggy driveway, around the outbuilding and entered, as Madeliene had already gone inside. She was standing less than ten feet away from him, not like the Madeliene in the dream or in prior reflections but much different. Her hair was blueish black, and shadows danced around her form, blurring her outline at times, and her dress was tinged-brown lace yellowed with age and mildew. Worse was the gaping wound in her neck, dark and radiating, dendritic marks along her frail neck and right cheek. If he had never seen her before, the appearance would have terrified him.

"I wanted you to see the real me...as I am now, JJ. No illusions, no tricks, but exactly what I have become. Maybe now you can understand how important it is to stop him. If we cannot, then I fear many others will suffer my fate, or worse. Tomorrow is the last day before the Split Moon begins to build. His powers will peak at midnight on the striking of the nine with the Split Moon. Worse, as his power grows, mine seems to be fading. If we can deny him his prize until then, I might be able to at last break the bonds holding him to this world."

"Don't worry about the stone, it's safe with the professor tonight. But what about you?" JJ asked concerned. "The literature says anyone who becomes a revenant will—"

Madeliene finished, with a hint of sadness, "...Be a monster too." She shook her head. "Truth is, I do not know what I am anymore or what will happen to me once he is gone. I will confess, having felt dark thoughts and emotions—intense anger, jealousy, even spite, yes. I struggled with these feelings in life and more so over the past few decades. But I have never acted on the worst, the never-ending hunger. It's my last shred of humanity, and I will not give him the satisfaction of taking it from me."

JJ started to subconsciously step towards Madeliene like in their dream to comfort her, but she held up her hand to stop him.

"Remember that I am still a revenant, JJ, and it is best you do not get too close. Ever."

"Oh right, the odor thing. Sorry, I forgot," JJ added sheepishly.

She almost giggled at his innocent response. "Sure that, but also that little thing called the darkness within me. You cannot understand how vile it really can be. It sits ever so patiently within darkest recesses of my being, collecting the tiniest details to use them against you. I call it the 'Joy Killer' because it takes pleasure from causing the maximum pain and suffering. Not only to me but everyone around me. It is forever, a relentlessly evil. I couldn't bear that for you. Because...you're a nice boy, JJ."

JJ replied defensively, "I'm not *that* nice, you know."

She giggled at his response. "Oh, yes you are." Madeliene glanced at the ground. "Can I confess something to you and only to you? Nothing bad, but embarrassing to admit."

JJ replied, "Of course you can."

"I've been watching you for several years. Not in a creepy way, mind you, but out of caution when you would come by my old house and help Mother. You always did so many nice things for her. Even getting Tommy and your father to help her at times."

"Tommy said he always felt like someone was watching us."

Madeliene lifted her gaze and added, "Sorry, bad habits, I guess. Tommy is tuned into the elements, and cute too. But you remind me of a boy I knew in my time called William. He was smart and learned like you. Oh, how I had the biggest crush on him. I think the other kids in town teased and called him terrible names for years, because he was small, smart, and always had a book with him. He had the cutest little silver-rimmed spectacles."

This was a memory JJ could tell clearly brought Madeliene joy. JJ asked, "Did you ever talk to him? William?"

Madeliene replied, "Once, briefly. He was in the grocery store and Mother was busy with the butcher. I told him his glasses were nice which made him smile; he said he liked my hair barrette. It was a simple, plain silver hair clip, a gift from my late grandmother, but my most prized possession. On impulse, I removed it and quickly placed it in his hand and told him, 'To bring you good luck.'" Her face shifted from happiness, flashed anger, and then sadness. "Of course, Mother saw us talking and rudely ended our conversation. I never had the chance to speak with him again, and after—well, you know, his family moved away too."

"I understand, Madeliene. I do. I've never been good at telling girls how I feel either. I want to, but my tongue gets dry and then I always chicken out."

"What about Ally?" she asked with a hint of surprise. "Thought you two were going steady?"

JJ smiled and laughed to himself. "No, we're not like that at all. I'm the brother she never had."

Madeliene pried, "You've never told her how you feel?"

"Oh, I did. Last year after a school dance, but she..." he paused and uttered an exasperated sound, "...doesn't feel that way about me."

She nodded in understanding. "Does she like boys more like Tommy?"

JJ replied, almost off-handedly, "Actually, she doesn't like any of the boys at school, or anywhere else, if you know what I mean."

At first, Madeliene seemed confused and thought for a moment before her face flashed with awareness. "Oh, I see."

"We're tight, Ally and me. But I keep her secret and give her a social cover. You know, it may be the year 2022, but her parents, and most of this town, aren't that understanding about these kinds of things." Realizing what he had revealed, said, "You can't tell a soul."

Madeliene smiled and replied, almost sarcastically, "JJ, who would I tell?" which surprisingly made them both giggle.

"Wait a second. I have a crazy idea." JJ walked over to his dad's cluttered workbench and began rummaging through piles tools and other supplies.

Meanwhile, Madeliene drifted over to his mom's workbench, littered with unfinished stain-glass windows and other glass works she sold online or at the county fairs. Madeliene stared at the art objects and said, "I envy you. Your mother makes such beautiful things."

He replied, "Mom's quite an artist. She always has more orders than time to complete them. Busy taking care of us, I suppose. Would you like to have one? Maybe one of the angels. Mom has about a dozen on the shelf and I doubt she would miss one."

Madeline took in the works a final time before drifting towards JJ, and said forlornly, "They are glass, and my touch would shatter them. She loves you, nevertheless, and that makes a family. Treasure it above all other things, JJ."

While Madeliene's attention was diverted, JJ had found and donned an old clothespin, pinching his nose shut, painter's goggles, and a pair of his dad's heavy, leather welding gloves. Afterward, JJ confidently walked back over within a foot, confusing her. He extended his right hand to Madeliene in friendship. "Don't worry. See? No smell, burning eyes— nothing."

She hesitantly accepted his hand in hers.

"You have risked everything to save my friends and me today. Least I can do is properly say thank you. I can sense the conflicting emotions, but Tracy was right. You, the Madeliene you, are not evil, and we're going to do whatever it takes to get you freed from this thing. That's what friends do."

Their eyes locked in a deep stare when she said, "I was wrong, JJ. You're much cuter than William."

The connection between them, as odd or even unnatural as it was, lasted only a few seconds, broken by Lena calling out:

"JJ? Mom said you need to get back inside and quit fooling around."

JJ initially looked towards his sister's voice, but when he turned back around, Madeliene was gone.

JJ removed the gear and met his little sister at the doorway, closed it behind him, and upon seeing the revulsed expression on his kid sister's face, started to smile.

"JJ, you really stink!" she exclaimed.

"I know, Lena. The trash was super funky. So, maybe you can give me a big old hug!"

She squealed while he chased her back into the house, laughing all the way inside.

***

By ten o'clock, JJ was in his bedroom upstairs with the lights off and cellphone silenced when Ally called him. He told her all about the lake expedition, the police and military presence around town, and that he also was on lockdown.

Ally told him, "Tracy is spending the night at her uncle's place in Clinton. The feeling in Tommy's legs has returned, so they're probably going to be discharging him in the morning and she wanted to be with him. She said the hospital is being shutdown anyway and needs to relocate their patients until the building can be repaired."

"What about her dad?"

"He's in a hospital in Kansas City but stable after surgery. Her mom is staying in town until Saturday." Ally paused before asking, "When did you say the professors wanted to meet up in the morning?"

"Around eight or so at the library. I was going to text Augie early but I'm carless, you and Tracy are on lockdown, and Tommy won't be back until later. The quarter moon or Split Moon begins tomorrow night and peaks Saturday. Means we'd better think of something to be able to meet up with them."

Ally said, "Maybe we can meet up at Tracy's once she gets back from Clinton. I know Tommy's parents will want him home, but it's Friday and my parents will be at the church all day preparing for weekend services. I'm sure I can convince them to let me hang with her all day after what she's been through. Maybe you can go over to Tommy's and patch the professors in remotely from the library?"

JJ laughed lightly., "Duh, a remote meeting. That's not a bad idea. I'll text them both first thing and set up the Robo-meeting."

"I'm glad the weird stone is with them in St. Louis tonight, though. Daddy said there's been reports of animals going crazy all over town and an entire flock of starlings, like two-hundred birds, fell out of the sky dead at the Dollar-Mart. It's almost like they know something horrible is about to happen," Ally cautioned.

"How do you think Madeliene fits into all this?" JJ asked.

"Oh shoot, I almost forgot! I had time to read the letters and looked through the photo's we collected yesterday."

"And?"

"Five of the six letters were correspondence she had sent Madeliene's father in late January and February 1945. They were sweet and so much in love, and it hit home for me, because she got married at seventeen and pregnant right before he shipped out. The Army must have returned her letters after he was killed in action in early March."

"Right, but we knew all that from the ancestry thing already," JJ said.

Ally replied, "But it was last letter and photos we hadn't seen. The last letter was sent to Mrs. Cross from Mr. and Mrs. Robert Cross, or Thomas Cross's parents. It was dated November 3rd, 1951 when Madeliene would have been only six years old. In short, they were cutting all ties with her. They said specifically, while they didn't blame her for their son's death, that was the war, they could no longer bear being around their granddaughter. They said the child was 'obviously unbalanced and generally made them uneasy.'"

"Wow, not harsh at all. So, what does 'uneasy' mean?" JJ asked.

"I don't know but it was some of the photos that concerned me. Most were typical baby or child photos of Madeliene."

"Maybe before her mother completely lost it," JJ said defensively.

"Sure, I would image. But it's the way Madeliene appears in all them. Like she was staring through the camera with such intensity. No happy or funny poses. No smiles or blurry movement. Even the baby photos, her demeanor was frozen without even a hint of joy in her eyes," Ally replied.

"The Joy Killer," JJ said, which made Ally say:

"What are you talking about?"

"Oh, it was something Madeliene said when she was here earlier."

Ally asked uncomfortably, "What? She was at your place tonight? When?"

"It's not a big thing. It was around eight o'clock. She wanted to warn me again about the revenant and Split Moon phase rising. She described the darkness it created as ever-present and called it the 'Joy Killer' that she despised."

"You mean a revenant exactly like her." Ally said flatly without hiding her suspicion. "Because at the end of this, no matter what happens, she is one too. And you heard what the professor said about them. It doesn't matter who she was in life."

"Sure, Ally, of course I heard him. But that's according to old literature. Who knows what parts are correct, misunderstood, or merely superstition? I mean, what does she need to do to prove herself? Afterall, she's saved Tommy, Tracy, and today Augie and me from that thing. She's even admitted about the darkness within and not to trust it and wanted me to see her for who she really was. Maybe it's not too late for her. Perhaps destroying the thing that turned her in 1961 will somehow set her free from a never-ending nightmare. Like, I don't know, her soul or something?"

"Oh, JJ," she said with concern, "you need to be careful here. I know that tone in your voice. You're not actually falling for her, are you?"

JJ hesitated and then said sheepishly, "I feel...I don't know...like I feel sometimes.

You know, alone. If that makes me an idiot, then so be it."

"You care so much about everyone. That's why I've always loved you, JJ."

"Like a brother, yeah I know."

Ally sighed. "I love you so much more than that, you dork. Just not the other way. If I could, I would. You deserve that too, and so much more. But not with her. Okay?"

"Sorry for dumping, Ally. I do know how hard it is for you too," he replied.

"JJ, think of this way. You always see the good in everyone. That's why Tommy, Tracy, and I love you. Maybe if some small part of Madeliene remains, it sees it too and draws her to you. I don't know. But I will say what I've been thinking for several days out loud. Maybe the 'Joy Killer' as she calls it, is somehow playing all of us."

JJ grumbled at her suggestion, but Ally interrupted his noisy protest.

"Please wait and hear me out. Remember, she warned us in her dream, and you again tonight, not to fully trust anyone, even her, because of the darkness within. Right?"

"Sure." JJ crossed his arms defensively.

"I'm only saying we need to be careful. Because we don't know for sure how much control that thing, or the thing she has become, exerts over her. I'm not sure she does either. I certainly don't know where Madeliene ends and the revenant begins, and it terrifies me. Tracy absolutely trusts her and probably Tommy too, but I never will. Call it my religious upbringing, intuition or whatever, but evil is evil. Friendly visage or not. I'm sorry if that disappoints you."

JJ sighed. "I understand, and I'm not disappointed in you. We're all good here." He yawned. "I need to crash but I'll text you in the morning after I hear back from the professors."

"Night, JJ," Ally said, kindly.

"Night, Ally."

Chapter 8 – Split Moon Rising

JJ's alarm clock woke him at six a.m. He rolled over and turned it off while checking the calendar. It was Friday April 8th. He lay in bed for about thirty minutes wracking his brain and muttering to himself, "Think, JJ, think! We're missing something." He revisited the week's events and every detail he could recall but nothing new came to mind.

Rolling out of bed, he grabbed his cellphone and texted Augie.

Are you back in town, Professor?

Staring at the text, marked "delivered," but after a few minutes, it still didn't show "read."

"Ah, probably driving." So, he decided to call Professor Tombs who, much to his relief, answered.

"Good morning, Mr. Duncan. Are we going to meet up today at the library?" the professor asked.

JJ replied, confused, "Didn't Augie talk with you last night about our plans for today?"

"Well, yes and no. He called me from his motel and told me about your eventful boat ride, locating the revenant's cairn and possibly its ship. I was so excited, I hardly slept a wink and spent part of the night gathering my notebooks, the arrowheads you found, of course, and some artifacts from Mound Seventy-Two that might help us to lock that thing back in its cairn again. I suspect the arrowheads were part of a lock and they need to be somehow reassembled to be effective."

"Sir, I hear road noise. Are you travelling with Professor McAdams?" JJ asked apprehensively.

"That's the 'no' part, Mr. Duncan," Professor Tombs added with a hint of his own concern. "During our call late yesterday, Augie said he had secured the stone, checked out of his motel, and was going to grab a quick meal in town, before driving back to pick me up. That was around six o'clock. I expected to see him by midnight, but he never arrived. I have tried calling him multiple times, but his cellphone goes straight to voicemail."

"So, you're driving instead?"

"Oh, heavens no. That would be a disaster of my own making. I have a nice undergraduate, Ms. Lacy Hinton, who moonlights for this thing called 'FreeRide.' Maybe you've heard of it? Of course, it's not free but the university typically covers my travel expenses. Anyway, I digress. She was kind enough to pick me up around five a.m. today and is driving me to River Rock, as we speak." His focus shifted again, and he added, "She's an art major, you know, but I promised not to hold it against her because she's really helping me out of a tight spot—."

"Sir!" JJ interrupted in growing frustration, "what about Augie? He has the thing with him, you know?" JJ said evasively, knowing the professor's cellphone was on loudspeaker.

"I don't know what to think, Mr. Duncan. Augie has always been a reliable peer and friend. It isn't like him, at all, to be unavailable and it certainly worries me. I will keep trying to reach him and call the university as well. Perhaps they can send someone to search for him. Regardless, I won't be in town for about..." he paused asking Lacy.

"Oh, you're talking to me? Okay. Hi. Ah, we should be there around ten or so, Professor...and JJ."

JJ placed his head in his hands in growing frustration. "I need to set up the meeting; we're all scattered due to what happened yesterday. Why don't we plan on talking around eleven o'clock, if that's acceptable?"

"Perfectly acceptable with me, Mr. Duncan. And not to worry, I understand your predicament right now with family and friends. I will go back to the library and set up my laptop."

JJ could overhear him asking:

"Lacy, are you by any chance familiar with something called 'Robo-Meetup'?"

JJ said tersely, "I'll talk to you later, Professor...ah, Lacy," and ended the call with an audible groan while an uncomfortable knot was building up in his stomach.

Suddenly, a thought occurred to him; he quickly dialed and after one ring, heard:

"911 Dispatch. What is the emergency, please?"

"My name is Jimmy Duncan and I live in River Rock. I need to reach Deputy Benjamin Talon with the Benton County Sheriff's Office, please. It's life or death, and he knows who I am."

"One moment, and please stay on the line," the dispatcher responded. After a minute, he heard: "911 Dispatch transferring you to Deputy Talon."

Seconds later, he heard:

"JJ? This is Deputy Talon. Are you alright?"

"We might have a way to stop the thing that attacked us at the hospital. But Tracy, Ally, and I are—well, sir, grounded."

Deputy Talon, sounding confused, asked, "So, exactly what did you need from me?"

"Sorry, please let me explain. One of the professors from Washington University is on his way to River Rock in a car. His name is Dr. Daniel Tombs, and he knows a lot about ancient cultures. His colleague is Dr. Walter McAdams. He's an expert on the thing we encountered in Clinton, or at least weird things like it. He was on his way last night to bring Dr. Tombs back to River Rock but never showed in St. Louis. They both have artifacts and information that may help us stop it. We are planning on having a meet up online but its nearly the Split...ah, first lunar quarter."

Deputy Talon asked, "And that means what exactly, JJ?"

"It means that as powerful as the thing was in Clinton, it's about to get a thousand times stronger tonight and maybe even unstoppable by tomorrow."

Deputy Talon replied, "Got it, son. I just texted you my cellphone and link to our emergency response commander. I want you to call the professor who's travelling and get his current location and send it right back to the ERC. We'll dispatch the Highway Patrol to find and provide him with an escort to town. Also, send us the route the other professor travelled last night, and we'll do our best to search for him. Meanwhile, I'm requesting we place an incident command station out at your place. Having an ICS there puts us closer to the source and a lot of help at your disposal."

"Okay, sure, but what about Ally and Tracy? They're both connected to this thing too, for what it's worth. They need to be here. Ally should be at home now, but I think Tracy will be returning from Clinton with Tommy and his family today."

"No problem. I know Ms. Denton's address and will send Deputy Baker over to pick her up, and I'll contact the Henry County team and have them escort Ms. Hillman to your place and get the Baskin family back home."

"Is there anything else I can do until then?" JJ asked.

"Yes. Tell your parents to stay at home and that it's going to get very busy out there soon. Very busy."

***

Ally, meanwhile, had woken up after journaling late into the evening. She checked her cellphone and saw one text from Tracy:

Tommy's better and coming home this morning, followed by three happy/crying emoji faces. It was past 7:20 a.m., but she'd heard nothing from JJ.

She jumped out of bed and went into the bathroom, turned on the shower, and slipped in for a quick rinse to start what was surely going to be anything but an ordinary day.

After washing her hair, Ally got out, dried off, and wrapped the towel around her wet hair. She slipped on her teal bathrobe and turned around to the sink to brush her teeth. Covered in steam, Ally grabbed a dry washcloth and wiped away the moisture. When she stared into the cleared mirror, she jumped back a step and muffled a scream, holding her hands to her mouth.

Staring back at her was Madeliene's visage. But unlike before, she was dead; eye's glazed over and the wound at her neck decayed, vile and spread across her neck and face like a plague.

"I'm sorry to have frightened you," Madeliene said in weak voice.

Ally, recovering from her shock, asked apprehensively, "What happened...? Your face?"

Madeliene replied, "I am diminished and nearly spent. But I saw into him again in a vision. He has the last stone and the artifact he needs is close."

Shocked, Ally replied, "But how did he get it? The stone?"

"It was the scholar. He gave it to him late last night and has been a willing servant for many years. A decade or more, at least. He unearthed the weapon years ago, kept its whereabouts hidden, and manipulated the other scholar into bringing it here today. It is a ruse."

"I've got to warn the others!"

Madeliene cried out, wailing in agony, her image twisting over in pain, and uttered through her torment, "It has the stones, a mass sacrifice of mortal blood or Blot that was created at dawn, everything it needs for tonight are here except for the weapon. It needs and fears it."

"What about you? You said it also needed you?"

Madeliene twisted once again, as if she was staving off another severe bout of intense pain with a veil of darkness radiating around her. "I am sorry, Ally... I was foolish and may have doomed us all. I let myself remember happiness for a split-second last night, with JJ. I was stupid but only wanted to remember what it was like to be alive again. He held my hand, my disgusting, decayed hand. The emotion overwhelmed me, and I felt love for the first time. The Joy Killer knew that too and used it against me. I am now forever tethered to the place where it dwells." Madeliene lifted her lifeless gaze to Ally with tears streaming down her cold, withered face. "I know now what my mother, rightfully feared...I am Deathly Alive." Then she vanished in a blink.

Ally was weeping too as she fumbled for her cellphone and called JJ. "Pick up, JJ, please, pick up!"

But before he could answer, she heard her mom's voice from outside her bathroom: "Ally! Why is Deputy Baker and another officer in our driveway?"

***

"GOOD MORNING, RIVER ROCK! This is KL94.8, The River, and you've got Bobby Redhorse rocking out your morning here in the lovely town of River Rock with the morning news and weather. But, oh my, what a morning it's been. We'll start with well, the weather. According to geniuses at the National Weather Service, it's supposed to be sunny but, for some reason, River Rock, and most of the lake in this area is trapped in an 'unforeseen inversion low.' Otherwise, FOG! Yes, my friends, another lovely day at the lake, blanketing us in that ever-depressing drizzle and fog. YIKES! Seems like we turned into Seattle. Next thing you know, there will be coffee drinking hippies everywhere.

"But hey, that's not all River Rock. We woke up this morning to find ourselves, and most of Benton and Henry Counties, it seems under Marshall Law. Yes, following the quote 'gas leak and explosion' at the hospital yesterday, there has been a growing presence of local, state, and some federal alphabets popping up everywhere between here and Clinton. Word is that sometime in the wee hours of the morning, an 'Emergency Command Center' or as I like to call it, 'Big Brother's Overreaching Grandstand,' was set up in River Rock to address a potential terrorist threat. Complete with the National Guard kiddies setting up check points all over town and along HWY 7. BUT I'M SURE THEY ARE HERE ONLY TO PROTECT OUR RIGHTS! HA!

"Wake up, River Rock! We knew something like this has brewing for a while. But don't worry, I have it on good authority that our patriotic and fearless militia, Nathan's Nationalists, led by local boy and my favorite cousin, Nathan Lee Baldwin, were ready. They mobilized their tactical teams late yesterday and were able to bypass big gov's checkpoints, establishing 'Freedom's Foothold' down by Old Town shore at the lake.

"Why, I have Nathan's lovely wife, Tammy, on the phone now. TAMMY! Great to hear from you! How's Nathan and our patriotic best doing this morning at keeping our Second Amendment freedoms secure?"

"Bobby, I don't know!" the woman replied in distress. "I've been calling Nathan and as many of the patriots as I can, but they don't pick up. None of them! Last I heard from Nathan, he said they had made it to the shore of Old Town but there were dead birds everywhere. Every animal they came across along the way had gone plumb crazy, even tearing out pieces of their own flesh, as if something were boiling inside them. They had to put them down and deployed their gasmasks in case the government is experimenting with chemicals again.

"Last time I heard from Nathan, he said something was moving in the fog near the Old Town shoreline and his boys had put up a defensive position and were ready for bear. Bobby, I know I heard gunfire, and then his phone's signal cut out. Lord, I think they're in trouble! I called the Benton County Sheriff's Office but all they said was they'd look into it."

"Sounds like the usual government double-speak to me, Tammy," the DJ replied for his listeners. "Don't worry, I'm sure our faithful out there in River Rock and surrounding areas will keep an eye out for our true patriots. In the meantime, and considering this morning's weather, let's start of our music fest to a tune from CCR, while we start our FRIDAY! Yes, indeed! Bad Moon Rising...AROOO!" the DJ howled as the music began.

"Tommy!" JJ exclaimed, waving frantically as his family's truck pulled into the ICS, or the emergency response compound that had since sprung up around both their homes and the road leading to Mrs. Cross's place and Old Town beyond. The National Guard placed several concrete barriers and posted track vehicles and Humvees guarding it. It resembled a scene from a bad sci-fi movie. The only exception was a line of about two-dozen yard gnomes spread out across the roadway like happy but weird little sentinels. Several large miliary tents were also pitched on both sides of the road, and police, emergency, military, and government folks were everywhere, and more gnomes posted at key locations.

As Tommy's parents and Tracy got out of the family truck and helped Tommy into his wheelchair, JJ smiled at his friend, who smiled in return.

"What happened? An alien phone home or something?" Tommy asked.

JJ laughed, gave him a big hug, and said, "I knew it had to be you, big guy. I could hear that idiot redneck blasting his garbage on the radio clear up to the house."

Tommy laughed. "Ah, that's old Redhorse's morning show. He's funny, and I like the music too."

Tracy asked JJ, "Is Ally or Professor Tombs here yet?"

"The professor and his driver are here, thanks to the police escort. Ally should be here soon too," he added with a strained expression and forbidding tone.

"What's happened? It's Madeliene, isn't it?" Tracy asked.

"Yes. Things aren't good. But we'll explain in the command center once Ally gets here. The professor is setting up now for everyone in the larger tent over by our out-building," JJ explained, pointing it out.

"Well, let's get to it, then," Tommy replied.

As Tommy's mom smiled over her shoulder, Tracy said "Oh, no you don't, Mister. Doc said bed rest for you. Period."

Tommy rolled his eyes at JJ and smiled. "Alright, Tee." He glanced back to JJ, adding with a wink, "I think she likes me."

Tracy said, "I'm going to help Mrs. Baskin get Tommy situated at home and I'll meet you at the big tent."

JJ walked back into the command tent. As he entered, he overheard Deputy Talon, the ICS commander, talking to someone at the emergency center in town.

"Yes, I heard his radio broadcast a few minutes ago too, Sheriff. Jack and I both have known Nathan Lee since school days and most of the numb-nuts that traipse around in the woods with him. They're harmless, mostly, but Nathan Lee was always a brick or two short of a full load."

"No problem, Ben," replied the sheriff to Deputy Talon. "We'll keep an eye out for them around town and along Highway 7, but I'm not letting anyone go down to the lake shore or Old Town. At least not until this blanket of fog lifts and we all have a better idea what the heck is going on down there."

"Roger that, Ted. The professor is here and setting up a link to your ERC as we speak. He should be ready to present his findings at ten."

"Good. I've got the district colonel from the Army Corps of Engineers tied in too, as well as National Guard unit commander, local fire department, County Health, River Rock Mayor's Office, and a CDC team from Kansas City. Hell, I even have the governor's office and a couple local state representatives online. It's an alphabet soup of folks on this end, Ben. Let's hope the professor can shed light on what's happening. ERC Commander, Henry County Sheriff Ted Dayton, over and out."

"Benton County Deputy Benjamin Talon, out."

He glanced up from the radio and spotted JJ. The deputy nodded to him while simultaneously reaching behind the table, handing JJ back his grandfather's shotgun and belt of unspent shells. "I think you left this behind in Clinton, if memory serves."

JJ accepted the shotgun, hung the shell belt over his shoulder, and said, "I saw the gnomes. Good thinking."

Deputy Talon replied, "Yep, they gave Deputy Baker and me quite an odd stare or two when we bought out the entire home improvement store. Made sure a bunch of them are at the ERC too. After seeing how well one worked in Clinton, figured best to get as many as we could lay our hands on."

JJ excused himself and ambled over to Professor Tombs who was being aided by a military IT technician and a young woman with short black hair who appeared like she could bench-press him, and her right arm tattooed from shoulder to wrist.

"Hey, Professor," JJ said.

"Ah, Mr. Duncan. Good to see you. This is Lacy Hinton. You spoke with her on the phone."

Lacy said, "Hi, JJ. Nice to meet you in person."

"Yeah, me too. Um, not to be rude, but, Professor, you said something about having some artifacts earlier."

"Yes. I've been going over my notes and am almost ready to present." The professor removed a handkerchief from his jacket pocket and wiped away perspiration from his brow, appearing excited but fatigued.

"Sir? Are you alright?" JJ asked.

He smiled at JJ and said, "I see you've been talking to Dr. McAdams about more than Scandinavian mythos. I'm fine but nearing my expiration date, it seems. The cancer started over a decade ago. Youthful indulgences I gave up too late. Treatment effectively sent it into remission for almost eleven years but made me quite ill during the chemo. Fortunately, Dr. McAdams, Augie, showed an interest in my work and really pitched in when I needed him. He finished the excavation at Mound Seventy-Two and has been there whenever I needed help. Especially during my current relapse." He gathered his composure, shaking off discomfort, and said, "I only hope he shows up today. I'm out of my expertise with Scandinavian cultures, let alone, the undead ones." The professor patted JJ on his hand. "Regardless, thank you for your concern, Mr. Duncan. If you could do me a small favor, please let Deputy Talon know I'll be ready in five minutes to discuss our findings."

A few minutes after ten a.m., everyone was linked from the ERC and elsewhere, while Professor Tombs started his presentation. He gave a brief background covering his decades of research, more recent collaboration with Dr. McAdams, and finally turned to the recent findings around the Old Town, the former church property, and what they believed was a burial cairn of an eleventh-century Norwegian ship. Afterwards, he discussed their experiences over the past week, with what could only be explained as a draugr from Norse mythology that had, for some reason, merged with the deceased River Rock resident from 1961 named Madeliene Cross, who was now either a spirit entity or another draugr.

When his presentation was over, he was showered with questions from many highly skeptical parties across the various government agencies and emergency personnel. At times, he yielded his conversation to JJ and Tracy, who had first-hand experiences with the entity and Madeliene.

Deputy Talon also provided support, based on his experience at the Clinton Hospital.

Suggestions followed from the "experts." A Colonel Jenkins from the National Guard said, "Seems simple enough to me. If this is really a monster of some kind, we have the firepower necessary and ready at Whiteman Air Force Base. I can call in an air strike in minutes and level that thing's tomb...ah, cairn, whatever."

Professor Tombs shook his head and said, "I understand how practical that action sounds, Colonel. But we have no idea what it kept within that structure besides other souls that were corrupted by it. Bombing it might entomb the entity or have the opposite effect."

Another colonel from the Army Corps of Engineers suggested, "Professor, how about we raise the level of the lake to summer levels. You said that thing hated water, right?"

The professor nodded. "That is a reasonable option, Colonel. How long will it take to raise the lake enough to resubmerge the area?"

"Sir, we can bring it back up in two maybe three days at the most. At least enough to fully submerge a structure at the coordinates you gave."

"I would recommend starting that process as soon as possible, but I don't know if it will happen soon enough to help this evening."

Deputy Talon asked, "Professor, could you please repeat at least what you suspect is going to happen tonight and how this thing is going to bring it about?"

The professor removed his spectacles, cleaned them, and said, "In broad terms, the creature entombed at the coordinates I provided is an undead entity called a 'revenant.' Think vampire, a physical being, with a Viking background but not limited by sunlight and can manipulate weather extremes. It can also change form or shapeshift from a small beast, like a trickster, to whatever is left of the warrior it once was or, when necessary, into a much more destructive beastly form."

"Exactly what hit us at the hospital," Deputy Talon added for support.

"Precisely. According to the literature, and my colleague, Dr. McAdams, it likely draws on supernatural forces associated with nine ancient artifacts it brought with it from Norway around 1,000 CE, called 'runestones.' My understanding at this point is such: the entity needed to be set free from its prison and succeeded at achieving that in 1961. It was, however, for luck or by intervention, re-entombed in 1979 due to the floodwaters of Truman Lake. With the unprecedented drought this past winter, the structure reemerged, and the entity began searching for one of the runestones that had been removed from its cairn unwittingly in 1961 by a young girl who lived nearby at the time—a Madeliene Cross. The same entity that apparently defiled her corpse and turned her into another revenant."

"So, now you're saying there are actually two of these creatures on the loose?" asked Mayor Thornton of River Rock.

"Yes, but it seems something within the Madeliene revenant has been at odds and at times assisting against the entity, once known as Red Eagle. We don't know why, or maybe it has something to do with her only being undead for over sixty years. No one can honestly say. What's certain is, this Red Eagle or revenant, needs the runestones, a powerful blot or blood sacrifice, Madeliene's spirit or soul, and another yet identified artifact. It plans to combine these things into a weapon of some kind at midnight tonight during the turning of the quarter lunar phase, or Split Moon, as it was called in his day. According to Professor McAdams, it must be successful at this task by the eve of April 9th, because the number nine has significance to its power over life and death."

He paused as multiple sidebar discussions broke out amongst the callers, giving him time to collect his thoughts, drink a sip of water, and listen to their responses. When the professor cleared his throat, he said, "Everyone, please. We know this for sure. The entity at this point only has its freedom and eight of the runestones. If we can deprive it of everything else, it stands to reason this creature will simply return to the cairn diminished at first light tomorrow, where we can hopefully seal it back in for good."

"PROFESSOR, IT HAS THE NINTH STONE AND MADELIENE!" Ally exclaimed, running into the tent. Everyone present turned to her as she walked up to the table where the professor, Tracy, JJ, and Deputy Talon were seated. "Madeliene appeared to me this morning in my bathroom mirror. She said it was Professor McAdams who gave it the stone and found the artifact it 'needs and fears' about ten years ago within that excavation in Mound Number Seventy-Two."

The expression on Professor Tombs seemed as if his entire world had crumbled out from beneath him. He sat down quietly and removed his glasses, again wiping the growing perspiration off his forehead while staring at his handkerchief. "It can't be. Dr. McAdams—Augie—is a true, loyal colleague and friend."

JJ asked, "But he still needs a blot, right? Blood sacrifice?"

Deputy Talon exclaimed, "Ah, crap! A local militia group has been missing since late last night. Probably around two dozen or so in the group if all of them were there."

Professor Tombs responded, "Not as many as were uncovered at the Cahokian mound but probably a suitable sacrifice nonetheless."

Ally added, "That's not all. Madeliene was dead, decayed, and lost. She said it has her, and she is truly Deathly Alive."

The professor dropped his spectacles, causing them to break when they hit the ground; he appeared to tremble. JJ and Lacy, steadied him for support.

JJ asked, "Are you alright, sir?"

"Water please, Mr. Duncan."

Ally knelt beside the professor. "Sir, I'm sorry to ask this, but did Dr. McAdams have you bring something with you today?"

The professor pointed to a case over on the other table. "Inside...inside the case."

Deputy Talon grabbed the case and brought it back to the table where the professor was seated. He scrutinized the professor, who nodded approvingly, released the metal catches, and opened the plastic container. Inside it was filled with oyster shells, but buried within them was an old sword made of iron with an ornate pommel laced with pure silver and embossed with the symbol of an eagle.

Professor Tombs stared at the buried sword in astonishment then back at everyone else. "I'm such a complete fool. Close the case, for God's sake. Close it!" His face became pale and etched with pain. He slumped forward where JJ and Lacy caught him.

The deputy grabbed his radio and said, "This is Deputy Talon. I need a medical team at the IRC tent ASAP!"

Meanwhile, JJ slammed the case shut and clipped the latches tight. He paused and, hearing nothing, uttered a sigh, but then the winds began to blow outside the tent, followed by the distant sound of rolling thunder. JJ grabbed the case and followed everyone outside.

To the west, the sky was boiling and churning like nothing anyone had ever seen before.

JJ said to Deputy Talon, "I don't think we have enough gnomes this time."

The deputy turned to JJ, Alley, and Tracy and barked, tossing them his keys, "GET IN MY CAR AND GET THAT THING OUT OF HERE, NOW!"

They ran over to his vehicle while Lacy pulled her car up and helped the professor get in.

Meanwhile, Deputy Talon radioed the incident guard unit captain, who had already pulled up every military vehicle present at the barricade, including four Humvees and several Bradley fighting vehicles.

"GIVE IT, ALL YOU GOT, CAPTAIN!"

When the storm poured over the last ridge, it shifted violently, streams of lightning cascading along the ground as it changed into a massive, nearly twenty-foot-tall bull-like creature driving straight at the checkpoint.

"FIRE!" the captain ordered.

Round after round tore through the field dropping trees and everything else in its path, except the approaching beast which only got angrier.

The captain stared briefly in disbelief and commanded into his headset, "Delta-Seven, Delta-Seven, this is Bravo-One, we need tac-air now at the coordinates I'm sending, over!"

In response, the recipient commander replied, "Bravo-One, this is Delta-Seven in route, please verify your coordinates are danger-close. Over."

To which the captain replied, "YEAH, AND WE DAMN SURE ARE NOT ALONE! BRING THE HEAT NOW!"

"Rodger that Bravo-One, the heat is on its way. Keep your heads down, Captain."

The entity was less than two hundred yards away from the military blockade when two A10 Gunships screamed by overhead and opened fire sounding like giant frogs in unison. The impacts of high-explosive incendiary rounds from their guns tore into the creature, rolling it to an abrupt stop in a torrential cloud of dust, dirt, and debris.

A cheer rose from the entire camp while some of the soldiers could be heard, chanting, "GO, WARTHOGS! GO!"

The creature recoiled in pain and retreated back through the woods, beneath the blanket of fog, along Old Cedar Road, and beyond their sight.

The captain slid back against his track's open hatch and, with a deep sigh, said, "Nice work, Delta-Seven. We owe you one, big time. Bravo-one, out."

Deputy Talon saluted the guard unit and grabbed his radio. "JJ, where are you?"

After few seconds of silence, Ally replied, "JJ's driving. We're almost back to town. Is everyone alright?"

"For now. But if this thing is getting stronger, I'm sure we're only going to serve to piss it off tonight."

"Deputy, we've had a change of plans. We're going to my dad's church."

"Ms. Denton? I thought you needed to get that artifact far away?" he asked, confused.

"We were speaking with the professor in the other car, and it's too powerful now. He's afraid distance won't prevent it from finding us and taking it. Our being out in the open travelling is too vulnerable. We figured it's best to go over to my dad's church. It's the town storm-shelter, and if this thing is anything like a vampire, well, maybe it can't come in or something like that?"

The deputy replied, "Alright. Ally. I'll call the ERC commander and have them secure a perimeter around the church and be right there. Stay inside and lock everything down tight, for whatever that's worth."

"Thanks, Deputy."

By the time they reached the church, the ERC team had secured the area and let them through. The church was surrounded by military vehicles and soldiers at multiple locations and stacking dozens of sandbags for quick placement of larger machine guns.

In the northwest, the fog was growing and moving south and eastward up from the lake and Old Town. It was nearly three o'clock, but it was already black as night.

Chapter 9 – Deathly Endings

"BEEP. BEEP. BEEP. The National Weather Service has issued a severe weather warning for eastern Henry and western Benton counties. Residents in these areas are advised to remain at home and, if able, take shelter due to a stalled inversion weather pattern that can produce precipitation and fog, lightning, and potentially damaging wind speeds. Visibility is limited due to the severity of these storms that appear to build up with little advance warning. Low-lying areas may also be vulnerable to flash flooding, and if in one these areas, residents are advised to seek higher ground and shelter. This has been a National—"

JJ turned off the radio.

Ally said, with relief, "Thank you, JJ. I always hated those loud beeps."

It was after six p.m. and dark while the town was fully beset by the pervasive ominous, thick fog that had stretched outwards from the lake like gnarled fingers. Lightning storms were raging along the lakefront and surrounding woodland areas.

Deputy Talon and dozens of National Guard unit soldiers were posted outside, and the church was locked up tight. JJ, Ally, Tracy, Professor Tombs, and Lacy had settled in as best they could and were going over everything they could think of, but mostly, hoping to simply wait out the night.

JJ said, "I don't think it knows where the artifact is, Professor. It seemed to get confused when we closed the case and left my house."

"The oyster shells, Mr. Duncan," Professor Tombs said with a weak grin. He was obviously feeling worse, demonstrated by the tremble of his right hand that had become far more pronounced.

"Professor, you're not well. Can we get you anything?" Lacy asked.

"I'm tired, that's all, Ms. Hinton. Maybe, I can lie back on this pew and take a nap to recharge this old man's body."

Ally said, "JJ, call the deputy outside and have them send in a doctor or EMT."

But the professor protested, "Nice of you to think of me, but do not open the doors for any reason. It may be our best hope at keeping it from finding us."

Ally grimaced with concern. "Well then, the least we can do is make you more comfortable. I know there are blankets and pillows in the supply room we keep for youth group sleepovers. I'll get them and stop by the kitchen too. We should all get something to eat, but especially the professor."

When she stood up from her pew, Lacy said, "Ally, would you like some help?"

Ally smiled and motioned for her to follow.

Tracy and JJ stayed with Professor Tombs.

JJ asked him, "Sir, what did you mean by the oyster shells?"

"As we discussed before, Mound Number Seventy-Two never fit well with the other mounds at Cahokia. Our excavations uncovered over two hundred bodies within multiple layers. Some had been buried alive near the base, some ritually sacrificed near the top, hands and heads cut off. While evidence of ritual sacrifice had been unearthed before at other Mesoamerican sites, nothing compared to this degree of violence. Anyway, near the uppermost mound a single man was interned. Maybe a chief or at least someone of significance. He was buried on a bed of thousands of oyster shells placed in the shape of a birdman or falcon."

"Like you said before in the library. The birdman has some religious importance for the area native culture," JJ said.

The professor grinned. "You get an A for listening, Mr. Duncan. Yes, indeed. Others always thought the shell motif illustrated 'the Birdman,' but what if it was a warning instead at this mound, and shells were there to hide what was really buried beneath? For instance, we now understand that Augie..." he paused as disappointment flashed across his face, "...Professor McAdams assisted me with the excavation of the lowermost chamber, where about forty persons were buried alive. During part of this work, I was indisposed, receiving chemotherapy, and Dr. McAdams was in charge. Current circumstances suggest he found the artifact in question during my absence and hid it at the university in our department's storage facility. He tagged the case in accordance with the corresponding mound but only identified it as containing oyster shells. I probably moved it dozens of times over the past decade and never thought once to inspect its contents, being more concerned with the trove of arrowheads, beads, and other items unearthed; some that match perfectly with the three arrowheads you discovered. Which reminds me, the arrowheads I borrowed are in my travel bag's outside pocket. Please, help yourself to them."

Meanwhile, Ally and Lacy had retrieved the blankets and pillows from the storage closet and were in the kitchen gathering some refreshments.

As she was rummaging through the refrigerator, Ally asked, "Lacy, are you one of Professor Tombs students?"

Lacy giggled and said, "Oh, God no. I had his class last semester, only because it was a required credit. I think he showed mercy and let me slide by with a passing grade. I'm an art major. But I do help Dr. Tombs whenever he calls. I feel sorry for him, being alone and all. Plus, the university pays me to drive him around town which helps pay my tuition."

Ally pointed to her arm and said, "Nice ink, by the way."

"Thanks. Some are my own designs. I do have a soft spot for roses. Shakespeare too," Lacy replied, pointing out a small ribbon with the words: *To thine own self be true.* "You have any ink?"

Ally laughed. "No. My dad is pastor here. Let's say, neither he nor my mom would ever approve," she added with a hint of frustration.

Lacy smiled. "I understand. I transferred to Wash U. from Marysville last year. Wasn't exactly a good fit for me either. That's the best part of going away to college, though. You don't have to let anyone tell you who you are, what to do, or even who you love. Oh, and I like your crucifix too; it suits you."

"Goes with the good pastor-daughter facade, that's all."

"Everyone's got a look, Ally."

In response, Ally blurted out, "I do like to write."

Lacy nodded approvingly. "Nice. What? Like fiction or nonfiction?"

"Nothing important, really. Sometimes I journal my day and thoughts but occasionally my dreams, wishes. You know what I mean?"

"I know exactly what you mean. That's what I do with my art and tats." Lacy smiled and softly patted Ally's hand. "Don't put yourself down, sweetie. You'll find your way."

She didn't really know Lacy, but her attitude, openness, and kind words made her somehow feel comfortable in a way she had never felt before with her other friends.

"Your boyfriend's cute, though. Seems like a total STEM guy to me, even packing a shotgun, but nice enough," Lacy added.

Ally giggled and replied, "JJ and I are just friends. He's available if you're interested. Although, I think you intimidate him."

Lacy laughed. "Oh sweetie, I was only making small talk. If I was interested in dating anyone around here, I'd be more interested in a dreamy writer with a shiny crucifix."

Her response left Ally speechless and fumbling for the juice boxes she had gathered.

Lacy grabbed the blankets and pillows under her arms and smiled. "Come on. We better get these back to the professor and the others. Hope I didn't make things weird for you, Ally. I'm an open book girl."

Ally collected her composure, picked up the groceries and juice boxes, and replied, "No, that's okay. I do like books."

They smiled at each other and strolled back to join the others, Ally with a lighter movement in her step.

Back in the sanctuary, Lacy and Ally made the professor as comfortable as possible, propping him up with a couple pillows and placing a blanket over him. They all had a juice, a few chips, and some peanut butter crackers Ally brought back from the kitchen. After a sip or two of his juice and few bites of food, the professor dosed off and, thankfully stopped trembling.

Other than light winds blowing outside, the church was unnervingly silent. JJ and Tracy sauntered back out into the vestibule to stretch their legs, while Ally and Lacy stayed behind to watch over the professor.

They both stretched, stiff from sitting in the pews, and pulled out their cellphones. Tracy started texting with Tommy, while JJ checked in with the deputy and the ERC team outside.

Tommy was resting in his bed at home when Tracy's text arrived:

Tommy, everyone safe?

Tommy responded: *Tee, man, it was pissed off!!! After you all left, storms tore up the hillsides back towards the lake...then bounced around all over the place down by Old Town...like a kid throwing a fit.*

Tracy replied: *It's been quiet here so far. Maybe it doesn't know where we are.* *Fingers-crossed emoji*

Tommy replied: *Best we keep it that way and short then, Tee.*

Tracy agreed: *Love you, Tom-Bear,* *heart emoji*

Tommy replied: *Same here, Tee, and back at ya*

He put the cellphone down when something heavy landed on his chest and stole his breath away. Opening his eyes as the smell of decay filled his nose, he was staring up at Madeliene leering over him; her left hand, planted on his chest, held him immobile. He tried to speak but could utter nothing.

She held her free hand's finger to her lips and said, "Shoosh. Hi, Tommy. Nice to see you again. Would you be a dear and loan me your little phone? I only need it for a minute and promise to give it right back." Madeliene picked up the cellphone with her right hand, studied it briefly, and said, "Oh, of course, I am so silly." She faced it back towards Tommy. "Smile for me, Tommy," using his face to unlock the screen. Turning it back to her, she smiled a dark visage, waved her hand that had been holding Tommy motionless, leaving behind a dark, cat-like creature on his chest which freed up her other hand. "Let's see if I can remember how JJ did it. Oh, there it is, my phone finder," and lightly tapped the app. Madeliene watched as the tracking app spun and located JJ and Tracy's phones. "Ah, back to where it all started. Nice touch. I so miss hallowed ground."

Madeliene got up from his bedside and carefully placed the cellphone back by Tommy as it shorted out. "Oops. Sorry, Tommy." She twisted the fingers on her right hand and made the darkness on his chest lift and vanish, allowing him to gulp, cough, and regain his breath. "You are a cute boy. But you were never my champion." And in a blink, she was gone.

***

Meanwhile, JJ, who had been talking with Deputy Talon, said, "Thanks again. We'll keep it locked up tight, for sure." He walked back over to Tracy while briefly glancing at the time on his cellphone. It was past 7:30 p.m. "Moon's rising, Tracy. We better get back in the chapel with the others."

Seconds later, both their cellphones sounded, as did Ally's from the sanctuary, but instead of their individual ringtones, all three played simultaneously "Ave Maria." Staring at their respective screens, each read "Madeleine."

"TURN THEM OFF! TURN THEM OFF!" JJ yelled. "It's her thing with reflections, remember. Don't go anywhere with a mirror and keep the blinds pulled down. It's reflections. That's how she moved around before and avoided the entity. Now that it has her, it must be manipulating her abilities to find us."

Tracy asked, "How did she find us? Ally, our tracking apps... TOMMY!"

JJ stopped her from turning her phone back on, and cautioned quietly, "You can't, Tracy. It will let her in."

The professor had woken up during the music and commotion, slowly rose from his pew, and secured the case and his small travel pack. "I think our hypothesis was right, Mr. Duncan. Like a vampire, she or it cannot come in unless invited or through an open doorway, like in a reflection."

An instant later, the power shut off, along with the rest of the town. At first, it was pitch-black, but then the chapel began to brighten with a radiant glow emitting from the baptistry pool by the room's entrance. The water began to boil as blueish light danced along its edges and spilled out onto the floor in a cascading display.

"JJ? Tracy? Ally?" Madeliene asked with a tone of malevolence.

"Foxfire!" Professor Tombs exclaimed.

Madeliene slowly rose from the torrent of water and stepped out of the pool, bathed in a blueish glow, and emitting the stench of decay. She stared briefly at a large crucifix carved into the stone fount, touched it with her slender, decayed forefinger, and held it for a few seconds. "Even now, in this sanctuary of faith, he remains silent to me. How predictable."

JJ stepped forward and unslung his shotgun, loaded it, and pointed it at her. She eyed him inquisitively, as he pleaded, "Please, don't make me do this, Madeliene."

A flash of sadness darted across her face. "I no longer have a choice, JJ. He can make me do anything...whether I want to or not." After, a brief silence, she said, "For instance," and clapped her hands together.

In response, the walls, floor, and ceiling of the sanctuary broke into tiny shards like the mirror in her bedroom, flinging in all directions and leaving everyone standing on an old country road, watching a mound in the distance as the fog parted above exposing the rising Split Moon.

"You need to follow us," Madeliene said flatly while multiple figures, like JJ had seen in the boat, moved menacingly around them.

JJ nervously fingered his shotgun and turned back towards the road behind them.

The professor put his hand on his shoulder and said, "No, Mr. Duncan. There are too many. Not yet."

JJ acquiesced and lowered his weapon.

They followed Madeliene along the muddy roadway which eventually opened to the remnants of an old stone country bridge, recently exposed from the watery depths of the lake. As they crossed it, the roadway beyond wound up a small hill and the source of the foxfire.

After Madeliene, JJ followed first, Tracy steadied and assisted Professor Tombs, and last were Ally and Lacy, equally terrified and staying close to one another. Along the winding road to hilltop, several dozen dead trees, stripped bare of their limbs from their watery slumber, were adorned with the remains of the missing militia members. Sacrificed with the telltale methods of the Blood Eagle, their entrails and ribcages piled at the base of each tree and the muddy roadway soaked red with blood.

JJ's eyes widened with horror. "Guys, for God's sake don't look up!"

Naturally, none could resist, and each had to stifle their cries of revulsion.

Reaching the end of the road and hilltop, they could see rotted and charted timbers torn aside in two large heaps as if something powerful had simply pushed the remnants of the old church foundation, driftwood and other debris aside. Exposing a single mound with a large fracture, split open in the side and the final source of the foxfire spilling out and illuminating the entire area.

Madeliene paused and appeared to be listening to someone while staring at the opening. She turned back to their captives and, without the slightest hint of emotion, said, "Remain here. It is almost time."

Ally cried out, "What? It's not yet midnight!"

Madeliene turned back to her. "I brought you here by dream-walking. Time is fluid in my dreams. I can make it go slowly as before when we met, or quickly. It is nearly midnight and the striking of the nine looms."

Professor Tombs wobbled but was caught by Tracy as he slid to a seated position, dropping his travel bag in the process and the case baring the artifact. Squinting, he fumbled for his bag, asking JJ, short of breath, "Mr. Duncan, my spectacles. If you would be so kind... I have another pair in my travel case."

JJ knelt, zipped open the small leather bag, and fumbled inside until he felt the glasses case he handed to the professor.

Professor Tombs opened the case, slipped out a pair of old, silver-rimmed spectacles, and donned them. He blinked and then stared in disbelief. "Much better. Thank you, Mr. Duncan."

As JJ was putting the glasses case back into his travel bag, he noticed the initials on the cover: "WDT." "Professor?" JJ asked calmly while closing his case, "what does the 'W' stand for?"

He smiled at JJ. "William. But I go by my middle name, Daniel. Never really liked the name; also back in my childhood, the other kids would make cruel rhymes with the moniker 'Billy.' You understand how cruel bullies can be sometimes." He smiled at JJ. "In truth, I also thought Daniel sounded a tad less stuffy than William."

JJ did his best to hide any feelings he was experiencing, but the older scholar must have seen something change in his expression and the memory Madeliene had shared only with him.

The professor abruptly stood up, dusted the dirt off his pants from where he was seated, smiled, searched everyone's expressions, and turned back to JJ. "She told you, didn't she?"

Ally, appearing as surprised as everyone else, asked, "JJ? What is the professor talking about?"

JJ stared at Professor Tombs with disbelief and said, "Augie is not the entity's servant. He is!"

The professor glared harshly at JJ and said, "Little late to help you now, Mr. Duncan. You get a D." He subsequently bent over without any hint of illness or tremor, grabbed the artifact case, and paused. "Oh, and before any of you misfits even think about stopping me, please remember his servants are all around and will tear you in half at my orders, shotgun or not." He opened the case, reached into the bed of oyster shells, and pulled out the sword by its grip, turning the blade in the radiating foxfire and smiled sadistically.

Shocked and repulsed, Tracy said, "You were playing us! What kind of man does that?"

"Why, a brilliant man, Ms. Hillman," he said with a sneer of delight. "Tell me, how's your dad and boyfriend doing? Hm?"

Tracy glared daggers at him while he laughed maniacally.

"Think you have it all figured out, don't you? Pathetic. Allow me to fill in a few key details to the storyline, eh, Ms. Hillman?" he said, turning back to Tracy.

"My family was there in 1961, you know. I asked my parents to bring me. To pay my respects to a girl I had met once in the grocery store. I wasn't there to grieve but to observe. I already knew what was going to happen; the day she had first encountered him, I later did too. You see, I saw Madeliene crawl out from under the church and waited until she and that idiotic reverend left, but too many people were around. But I managed to return the next day without being seen and crawled beneath. He was angry, as was I... Bullies were particularly cruel that week. But he understood and even showed me his past."

"He's a monster!" Ally exclaimed.

"Perspective, my dear sweet Christian child. Let me ask you this: How would you react if you had been out travelling, and when you returned home, found your parents, wife and children crucified, along with everyone else in your village simply because they wouldn't surrender the old ways? That was the day Erik Flett was undone and Red Eagle was born. Thanks to the real Christian experience. First the soft sell, or God loves you, blah, blah, blah. Then condemnation. You'll burn in hell, oh no! And when that fails, they brand you as a heretic and the hard sell follows. They kill you as an example or to save your poor soul. Note, the last method has proven rather effective over the past two thousand years at converting followers. Also, conveniently lets them take all your worldly possessions which is what it has always been about—plain old greed and power." The professor walked around the group, sword in hand and then pointed at each of them. "I know everything you know—well, except for Ms. Hinton. She's only an idiot art major who drove me here."

She glared at him and said, "Lucky you're holding a sword, you wrinkled, old prick."

He laughed. "Her honesty is refreshing, though. Certainly beats all the bootlicking students I've had to suffer through in the past. But, I digress, and time is short. Allow me to fill in a few more gaps in your understanding of this past week."

"Why would we believe anything you have to say?" Tracy uttered with disdain.

"You still don't get it, do you, Ms. Hillman? I know everything you know because Madeliene isn't your sweet, misunderstood bestie. He turned her decades ago and knows everything she thinks, hears, and sees. He is the 'Joy Killer' and everything he knows he subsequently shares with me. Oh, she tried to warn you all, not only once but multiple times, and congratulations, you ignored her like complete fools. Ms. Denton was close to getting it, but one last push, a dramatic final warning from poor Madeliene, and we had you completely onboard."

He moved over by Madeliene, who was blindly staring like a sentinel towards the cairn, as if waiting for commands. "Look at her. Does she appear to be in control? Ha! All her little plans, schemes, and manipulations were betrayed every time." He turned back to Tracy. "You know how the revenant can shapeshift, right? Three forms. The trickster or cat, its undead self, or the raging elemental bull. All revenants can appear as themselves, and eventually, with practice, take the form of the trickster. The elemental stuff comes much later and varies but it takes them centuries to master the raging storm, and Red Eagle has not taken the form of the trickster since 1961 when he enticed Madeliene into his cairn. Curious, don't you think?"

Tracy instinctually rubbed her chest as surprise flashed in her eyes, as well as in Ally's and JJs.

The professor smiled and said, "Now you know. It was Madeliene who contacted you first and hurt you. Oh sure, part of Madeliene thought she was working her little scheme to undermine it all, but she was also unwilling and, at times, an unknowing participant. At Mr. Denton's house, the Baskin's farm, and at the high school pool. She even paid her dear old mother a visit on the New Moon. All her."

"She saved Tommy," Tracy protested.

"No. But she did nearly kill him and thought she had. Impressive, because most revenants cannot channel their rage for centuries to take that form. It was all her. Split personality throughout everything," he corrected. He smiled at Madeliene, snapping his fingers in front of her lifeless gaze. "I think, at times, she almost believed it too. The darkness conceals so much from the light. No, I'm afraid the only part that wasn't her was at the hospital and earlier today. That's all him." He pointed to the cairn with a bizarre tone of admiration. "And you haven't seen anything yet."

"How did you get the last runestone? And where's Augie?" JJ asked.

"Simple really. You told her he had it. You know…in the barn when you both got all warm and fuzzy."

JJ burned with a mixture of rage and embarrassment.

"You told her. He told me. I called Augie en route and asked where he was at. He told Madeliene to retrieve it and she did without hesitation."

"And what of Augie?" JJ asked angrily.

"Tragically, his car plunged into a ravine after being hit by a freak lightning storm. Can't tell you if he's alive or not, and frankly, I don't really care. He served his purpose. Oh, and she also polished off that vegetable, Josiah Rite. But not his old-time pal, Mr. Jay. That was him again. You see, he always held a grudge for providing the kerosene back in the day."

Ally held her hands up to her face and began to weep, while Lacy hugged her for support. "You are such a vile, little man!"

"Oh, neat. The girls are getting along nicely. Maybe you should worry less about me and try telling Pastor Daddy how you really feel, you know, about boys. Bet old Dad would love to have that conversation."

JJ felt rage building within and said, "So what's in it for you? I mean, I get it. They stole your lunch too many times in third grade. So what? Think I haven't been there too?

The professor glared sideways at JJ. "Ah, Mr. Denton and I have something in common besides brains. I'll answer your question with one word: Immortality! When he gets this artifact, the cairn will shatter and release everyone inside. All his loyal followers and the buried ship will be restored, and they are going to cut a path of blood through this miserable continent straight back to his homeland. And nothing will be able to stop him." He turned back to Ally. "Tell me, Miss Denton, our little misunderstood Christian waif, do you believe there is a God?"

"I don't know," she said flatly.

"Ah, honesty again, so refreshing from the youth these days," he replied while examining the sword gleaming in the moonlight. "The locals did a fine job making this little item for him, at least until they figured out he really wasn't the Birdman. Not their God. Pity, though. It's never been consecrated." His wrist gracefully whipped the blade around, slicing cleanly through the teen's clothes and abdomen without pausing. "That's so much better."

The blade was razor sharp. JJ saw the motion, blood on the sword, and then overwhelming pain that dropped him wordlessly to the ground.

Ally and Tracy both screamed, "JJ!" as the professor calmly walked away towards the cairn's entrance.

"Oh, and to answer you, Ms. Denton, by this time tomorrow, I can assure you there will be a God." The professor glanced up at the sky, listened briefly, and said to Madeliene, "Tell him it's time."

As Madeliene walked towards the vile opening, Tracy shouted "Madeliene, I don't care what he said! We will always be your friends!" But Madeliene didn't react and marched away obediently into the cairn, regardless.

Lacy dropped beside JJ, pulled off her tank top, and started tearing it into strips. "We've got to put pressure on the wound or he'll bleed out. Ally, hold him still, and, Tracy, help me put pressure on the wound, here."

There was already so much blood. JJ was losing consciousness and had begun to turn pale.

Seconds later, Madeliene reemerged, and it was directly behind her—Blood Eagle. A massively imposing decayed remains of a man nearly seven feet tall, broad, dark, and vile. The smell of death whirled in horrid wisps around him; helm and armor covered in fresh blood and visceral from the day's earlier sacrifices.

Everyone was helplessly frozen in terror, wanting but unable to flee as it moved beside Professor Tombs, who dropped to one knee presenting the artifact: the sword.

It grasped the blade and turned it several times, admiring the weapon, and began uttering in an ancient language none of them understood. When it stopped, the revenant held the blade aloft, pointing at the Split Moon and said nine words. At the last utterance, the nine vengeance stones appeared before him floating in a circle, and each ruptured releasing a greenish vapor that flowed over the blade etching it with nine runic symbols.

Blood Eagle was pleased. It turned to Madeliene and said, "Gamall Blar, Gamall Blar, Gamall Blar," and held the blade once again aloft, positioned precisely between the light and dark of the split in the moon. The response was a tiny sliver of light that shined upon Madeliene, causing her visage to blur, and it began extracting her soul into the blade.

Ever the arrogant professor, Dr. Tombs laughed and retorted, "At last you understand, stupid waif. You are Gamall Blar. Your soul is key. You are his blood and immortality! And soon will be mine too." He moved around beside her where he could better observe and further gloat. "I was never your William. You were a silly girl, born with Old Blood. And I was just the means to get you to this very juncture. He reached into his pocket and retrieved an aged hair barrette. "I mean, did you think this silly, insignificant trinket would ever make any difference?"

The barrette, however, sparkled in the moonlight, then flew from the professor's surprised grip and attached itself to the blade where it melted instantly into the glowing metal. The artifact suddenly developed a life of its own, twisting in the revenant's grip before sending a violet pulse of energy downward. Like a massive electrical charge, it blasted the entity back into its cairn; the blade dropped with a re-sounding *clang* to the ground, runes fading away.

With lightning reflexes, Madeliene spun and grabbed Professor Tombs by his jacket, lifting him off the ground as he struggled weakly.

He could only utter, "How?"

Madeliene replied, "William, William, William. I'm glad you remembered that day in the store when I placed my barrette in your hand." She held him steady with her left hand, then released her right while pointing to her temple. "Visions, Silly Billy," Madeliene added sarcastically. She glanced sadly to JJ, who was nearly unconscious with a tiny tear rolling down her lifeless cheek. "I'm sorry, JJ. But I absolutely must break my promise."

She plunged her teeth into the professor's neck, as he screamed in agony while the dark and vile stain that had laced across her face and neck flowed downward to her lips and into the professor. He twitched and kicked, body thinned, turned dark, and eyes glazed over. When finished, she dropped his corpse to the ground, twitching, writhing, and stained with the mark of the undead.

"Don't worry, William. It's only the Deathly Alive. You will get the hang of it in few decades."

Madeliene was restored. She waved her arm in a circle and a ripple of violet energy swirled, pulling a stunned Deputy Talon through, while uttering, "What the hell?" as the earth trembled all around them.

The top of the mound subsequently exploded, showering dirt, stone, and artifacts everywhere. But Madeliene stood firm and her essence shielded everyone behind her as she snatched the sword from the ground which began to glow once again.

Blood Eagle was in full power, a twisting raging inferno, shifting back and forth uncontrollably from storm to beast, pounding the ground like thunder, uttering vile and dark commands, driving his servants surging towards them to recover his sword.

Madeliene raised the blade, made an arc in crackling violet energy, and yelled, "DO YOU REALLY DESIRE TO BE HIS SLAVE FOREVER? OR FOLLOW THE TRUE EINHERJAR!" and tossed the blade to Deputy Talon.

Catching it reflexively, the sword's runes lit up renewed with an intense glow that radiated down his arms and began pulling darkness from within Blood Eagle. It required every ounce of strength Deputy Talon could muster to keep holding onto the blade as the revenant wailed and diminished back into its undead form.

In response, his long dead followers turned and grabbed their former leader and held him motionless as he cursed them. "I AM YOUR KINSMAN! WE ARE OF THE OLD BLOOD! I AM NOW AND FOREVER BLOOD EAGLE!"

Instinctively, Deputy Talon charged and swung the blade in a wide and deadly arc, cleanly severing the revenant's head from his shoulders. Its body collapsed and a vile, steaming, dark liquid poured out into the soil where it fell. The undead host, all twenty-six of them, immediately crumbled into dusty piles of ash, fragments of bone and bits of corroded metal, while a unified voice was heard by everyone there that dissipated with the wind, "Frelse."

As the ancient weapon crumbled into dust, the deputy asked, "What did they say?" while his radio suddenly worked again.

"Ben, can you hear us? Over."

Ally called to him, "Deputy, help! They cut him."

The deputy ran over to JJ and the others. In all the chaos, Lacy had managed to stop the bleeding, but JJ was going quickly into shock from loss of blood and she told the others to lower his head and put their jackets under his feet to elevate them. "We've got to keep his blood in his heart."

Grabbing his radio, the deputy called, "Ted, I can hear you. But I need the standby Med-Air lift team down here at the lake by Old Town shore, ASAP. The Duncan boy is wounded and going into shock."

"Med-Air team heard you and is firing up. Should be there in two minutes. What about the thing, though?"

"Tell everyone it's toast."

"Rodger that, Ben! Nice work! ERC team leader, out."

Madeliene stood quietly, observing everyone, then answered the deputy, "They said 'free' like my mother used to in her native language."

Tracy glanced up from JJ and walked over to her.

Madeliene stared timidly at Tracy and said, "I wanted so badly to tell you... I've been naughty all along, so I won't blame any of you for hating me."

Tracy smiled and said, "But then it would've known too, and I understand that now."

Madeliene smiled. "After everything I've done, you wish to remain my friend?"

"Absolutely. Friends don't ever quit on one another." Tracy said before glaring back at the revenant's remains and the twitching, undead body of Professor Tombs. "It's not destroyed, is it?"

"Not yet. I believe you need to cremate them and dump the ashes into water. But I recommend asking Professor McAdams tonight; he is the expert on these things."

Tracy smiled. "He's alive?"

Madeliene nodded and replied, "I did not hurt him too badly, but he will need help. You can find him trapped in the wreckage of his car in a ravine about two miles south of Sedalia on Hwy 65, off the northbound lanes."

Tracy shouted to Deputy Talon, who overheard everything and was already on the radio, calling in the professor's location. Hesitantly, Tracy asked the obvious question, "But what will happen to you?"

Madeliene's expression changed to serious. "I'm tired and only want to go home. Take care of Tommy, Ally, and JJ. Friends are the real treasure." And in a blink, she was gone.

A light breeze blew, lifting the fog away and from within the dust of the former weapon, the glint of a small, aged silver barrette caught Tracy's eye. She bent over and retrieved it.

JJ survived his wound. Fortunate for him, Lacy had been pre-med before switching to art and kept him from bleeding to death, until the Med-Air team arrived, got him stabilized, and to a hospital in Kansas City. He was soon recovering not too far down the hallway from Sheriff Hillman's room.

Deputy Talon personally made sure the remains of Blood Eagle and Professor Tombs were sent directly to the nearest crematorium in the state. On Dr. McAdams advice, after he was rescued, of course, the remains were flown by charter plane to the coast and dumped unceremoniously into the Atlantic Ocean.

***

Saturday April 9th was almost over. Tracy, Ally, and Lacy, much at Tracy's urging, visited the old Cross place one last time. It was serene and no longer left anyone with a feeling of being watched.

Ally asked, "Do you feel anything, Tracy? I don't."

Tracy shook her head. They walked throughout the house, into the garden out back, and finally by the little dock on the pond in front. Though rundown, the place felt peaceful, and the previously barren honeysuckle was now blooming and laced the breeze with a joyful sweetness.

"Tracy, I think she's gone." Ally subconsciously grabbed her crucifix, for real this time. "I'll say a prayer for her," and meant it.

Tracy smiled with a mixture of sadness and joy. "I know, Ally. Can I have a minute to say goodbye?"

Ally clasped Lacy's hand tenderly and said, "We'll meet you back at the car."

As they walked away, Tracy stepped carefully out onto the old weathered dock. The setting sun was reflecting on the water and illuminated the vale in its golden beauty. She absorbed the moment of serenity while the sun slipped below the horizon and beneath the slowly fading light of the day. A warm April breeze blew gently across her face, and she heard laughter from across the pond.

Shading her eyes from the setting sun's glare, Tracy saw a young girl, maybe all of five years old, with dark hair and a pretty, lacy white dress. She was running along the bank of the pond giggling and chasing after a strapping young man and woman. Falling into each other's arms, they laughed and then glanced towards Tracy. It was Madeliene and her parents. They smiled and waved to her.

Madeliene held their hands firmly and mouthed: *Thank you.*

Tracy cried with joy, and replied, "You're welcome."

They ran off, once again laughing, and faded away with the setting sun.

"You're free, my friend."

She sniffled, wiped the tears from her eyes, and produced the old barrette from her pocket, placing it down on the dock.

Tracy stepped away and returned to her friends at their car. "Let's go. I need to get back and check-in on Tommy."

They pulled away and back down Old Cedar Road, as the first wisps of darkness began to creep into the vale. A light mist slowly lifted along the pond's reflective surface while the day gave way to night and the water began to cool.

As the clouds parted, the Split Moon appeared once again in the sky, but this time, it illuminated a young teenage girl with dark hair held fast by the returned shiny silver barrette that sparkled with a pale violet glow, standing alone on the dock. She gazed up at the sky and the ever-darkening night, while watching the stars come out and twinkle.

Madeliene smiled at the serenity and replied, "Whoever said I wanted to be free, Tracy?" With her utterance, all life teeming around the pond went deathly silent.

The End.

9 798888 120415